El Pagano

and
Other
Twisted
Tales

RD Armstrong

© 2008 by RD Armstrong
© 2008 by Claudio Parentela
ISBN 978-1-929878-98-7

Lummox Press
PO Box 5301
San Pedro, CA 90733

The author wishes to thank Chris Yeseta for helping with the layout, Claudio Parentela for the illustrations (www.claudioparentela.net/) and the editors of the following for previously printing some of these stories. **Dirt** (The Manx Tales) appeared in *Bender #2*, **Carl** appeared in *Aliens Are Real 4*, **Art Fag** appeared in *Last Call: The Legacy of Charles Bukowski*, **Cockfight** appeared on the *Assorted Realities* website, **The Manx Tales** appeared on *The Ragged Edge* website and was published in booklet form by the Lummox Press in 1999, **El Pagano** was also published by Lummox Press in 1998 as part of the *Little Red Book* series.

Cover painting by Tareq Swenson

Printed by CreateSpace.com

Table of Contents

Introduction

Many years ago, when I first started writing poetry seriously, I was advised by a friend that if I really wanted to be taken seriously as a writer, I'd have to write fiction because as she put it "anyone can write poetry." Well, over the years I've come to understand that while anyone can write poetry, like any other field of expression, some are better than others. So I dabbled at writing fiction, but my heart wasn't really in it...so much verbiage just to get a point across. I preferred the poem, where things could be suggested without going into great detail. A chair could be just that, or a chair could become a metaphor for something entirely different. It was clean and simple.

Over the years, as I continued to write poetry and essays (for a magazine I published for eleven years called the LUMMOX Journal), I also wrote more stories. With time it got easier and easier. Funny thing is, I don't believe I ever shared any of them with my friend, who'd started me down this path in the first place. As a poet, I had no qualms about sharing my work with anyone who would listen, but I was much more cautious about sharing my stories. Perhaps this is because, in the beginning, I wrote about what was most prominent in my mind: sex. Except for the last story in this collection I really haven't included any of the original "blue" stories that got me going, so to speak. Eventually, I settled down and began to write *stories* instead of sexcapades. Perhaps, someday, I'll publish these blue stories, though I'm beginning to think that life is already pornographic enough...

As to the title of this collection, the term El Pagano is a Spanish pun used by Gypsy performers. Literally it means The Pagan, or non-believer; but it can also mean The One Who Pays. A Flamenco guitarist once told me this story: when the Gypsies come to town to perform, they must find someone they can trust to make sure they get paid. Of course they don't really trust any non-Gypsy (or in their eyes, a non-believer in the Gypsy ways), so it's really a case of finding the one who is least likely to screw them out of their money. So El Pagano becomes an unlikely go-between...a role I've found myself in many times.

What the reader will notice in these stories is that the author, like the protagonist in each story, is definitely bent, if not completely broken. I make no apology for this. I am, after all a product of these demented times we find ourselves living in.

RD Armstrong
Long Beach, CA

ART FAG

The first time I met him, before he said a word to me, he handed me a business card which read (and I kid you not):

Sheldon Van Clam, Esq.
Poet-King of San Pedro
Patron of the Arts
By appt. (310) 555-3210.

It wasn't like he thought he was God's gift to the human race; but, rather, that we were God's gift to him. We were the toys sent to entertain him while he struggled with the weighty issues that plagued the planet; or, at least, his corner of it.

He'd say things as if they were slyly witty, even if no one else got the joke.

"The world is my oyster. Can I help it If I only remember this when it's out of season, heh heh heh?"

And then he'd laugh. It was a smug laugh. The kind of laugh that let it be known that he was on the inside track, and you weren't; that he was always going to be a winner and you were always going to lose, because it was his DESTINY!

He lived in an apartment house over on Sixteenth and Grand. He called it "Grand Manor". His 'auntie' owned the building and he was very tight with the manager. In fact, he was tight with most of the tenants, as well. They all thought the world of him too. It was a regular love fest! Life was grand over at the "Grand Manor".

Once, he invited me over to his apartment, back in the days when he thought that I might be someone he should know. The place was huge, almost palatial! Everything was neatly arranged, every piece of memorabilia, a testament to his greatness. There were letters of congratulations hung on the walls; each one in its own simple black lacquered frame. The signatures of many famous celebrities graced these pages. There were also numerous photographs of him with some of these same celebs: actors and the like; all smiling smugly, in that same way that I had seen him smile.

Across one wall, which ran the length of the apartment, there were bookshelves loaded with his 'Grand Archive'. It looked like a library starter kit! All the big guns in literature were present, as well as, the more popular names in fiction. He had the 'correct' books from the classics on, just about every writer that I had ever heard of and then some. Philosophy, Religion, History, Poetry and Prose, all were represented. It was all very impressive! I started to pull one of the tomes out and inspect it, but he stopped me, putting a surprisingly frail, but cool hand on me wrist. It was like being touched by a porcelain doll.

"I've spent many years building this collection and I'd be happy to share it with you, but, first we should get to know each other better, don't you agree?"

Somehow, I didn't like the sound of that. I didn't like the patronizing tone of his voice. He spoke to me as if I were a child; as if I would have to earn the right to gaze at the wonder of his treasures; as if I would have to be initiated into a secret society. A momentary vision of some pagan ritual involving children and a homosexual act danced across my brain pan. I shuddered.

He was a writer, or so he claimed. I read his stuff, but could make neither heads nor tails of it. I wrote poetry, which was easy, at least that was what all the fiction writers that I knew had told me. I didn't find it to be so in the beginning, but, with practice it got easier. Over time. But it was never what I would call easy. Unless you were a masochist. Poetry, for me, was always a painful process. And the poems that were the best were born out of much pain, usually a past memory that was sparked by some recent event, jogged loose by something that would seem to be too insignificant to even think about.

He was always giving advice. Change this word here, or eliminate that line there. He thought that I had potential. He wanted to be my patron, my agent. I knew he wanted a piece of me but it wasn't clear to me just which part or how much he really wanted. I didn't really want to find out, either. I wanted to get away from the bastard, but he'd hooked me with a few grandiose gestures.

Once, he'd given, not loaned, he was very careful to stress this, me enough money to pay off some debts and buy some time to work on my writing. Another time, he'd given me a Bukowski hardback, something that I never could afford, that was also signed by the author! I was touched by this generosity, but that was soon erased when he informed me that Bukowski was nothing more than an over-rated booze hound and whiner.

"Yeah, so what if he was?"

"Well, that's nothing; if you want to read the drunken ramblings of some alkie clinging to the skids! Me? I'd rather read someone who's going to challenge me; you know, make me think! Someone like Mailer or Updike! Blah, blah, blah."

And he was off on another tangent about the importance of being "true" to one's craft, of following a dream, of not getting distracted by earthly vices.

Claudio Parentela

Obviously, he'd missed the point that Bukowski had made. There was no dream; only a nightmare and the so-called "earthly vices" were a hedge against the inevitable insanity that one would experience as a result of said nightmare, and, of course, the purveyors and keepers of the "flame", so to speak.

That's when I began to hate him. I hated him even more, knowing that I would probably end up working for him, because he had plenty of dough and he knew that I needed money to survive. Worst of all, he would play at buying my friendship, because that's the way these things are done. Even though there was no way in hell that I'd ever succumb! I was his toy mouse. He played me like an unseasoned guitar player would, all technique, but no soul. It was all just a ruse, a way to kill time.

So it came to pass that one day, I ended up doing some work around his place, something to do with cleaning the bookshelves, I think. He had watched me climbing up on the pathetic little foot stool and standing on tiptoes to reach the top shelf. It was hot, sometime in August, and I was wearing some cut-offs, that were cut pretty short. I sensed that he was taking an interest, perhaps a bit too keen, in my actions as I strained to clean off the books and memorabilia.

"My goodness it's getting hot in here! Aren't you hot? How about a nice, cold drink?"

He headed towards the kitchen. I could hear him clinking around in there, fussing about.

A few minutes later, he called me out to the atrium for a break. He was the only tenant in the building to rate an atrium off of the breakfast nook in the kitchen.

"Sit down," he gestured to a chair across from him.

I sat on a stool at the bar. He tried not to be obvious, but he was staring up my leg.

"Here it comes," I thought, remembering that vision that I had had.

But nothing happened. He never made his move. He simply sat there pretending not to look and, all the while, unable to look away. It was pathetic! Worse, still, was the growing sense that I was finally in the driver's seat with this weird little man. I was actually beginning to enjoy this torture that he was going through. Maybe I could work this to my own advantage!

I finished my drink and headed back to the "Library" to continue to work. He didn't come in right away.

When he did return, he was agitated. He stood next to me and began to lecture me on "man's noble purpose" and moral responsibility and what not, all the while trying to look up my shorts! He was working himself into a real lather. I wasn't worried, though, I knew I could take him, if I had to.

Then he left again, bumping into a chair and mumbling incoherently as he exited. He didn't return. When I finished cleaning, I went looking for him. I called out his name, but no one responded. I searched from room to room. Nothing.

Then, I reached the very back of the apartment, the last room, which I assumed was his bedroom. I tapped lightly on the door and spoke his name as I entered, cautiously.

"Sheldon?"

The room was a complete disaster area. It looked as if a bomb had been exploded in there. Clothing lay on the floor and there was an unmistakably stale odor of decay hanging in the air like the memory of a love gone dangerously awry. As I surveyed the room, I noticed that there was also evidence of some truly fine, fast food dining; pizza crusts, boxes, crumpled hamburger bags, taco plates, wrappers. If we weren't on the top floor, I'd of thought that a garbage truck was using this room as a transfer station! My God! Am I still in the same apartment? A quick look down the hall confirmed this, but who the hell lived in this room? Visions of Norman Bates' mother tip-toed across the back of my mind. Geezus!

Then I heard the sound. It was the sound of whimpering and it was coming from behind one of two doors that were located next to each other at the rear of the room. By the white tile that was visible underneath the door, I figured that this must be the bathroom. Inside the door, I could hear someone crying, very softly. I was about to speak, about to offer some words of condolence, when I heard another sound that I was all too familiar with. It was a steady, rhythmical sound that, as a bachelor, I had come to know quite well. Flurp, flurp, flurp, flurp. I backed away from the door, quietly.

Most every man knows the solitude and frustration of jacking off into a sink in the cold, white harshness of a lonely bathroom. Staring into a mirror at yourself, at your face and then, at your meat, as you mechanically attempt to "clear the pipes". I've been down that road more times than I care to admit. But, at least, the spell had been broken!

Now it was I who had unmasked mister "high and mighty"!

I headed back into the living room, stopping off in the kitchen to make a roast beef sandwich and grab a beer. I plopped down on the couch and took in the splendor, as I downed my brew, Bukowski-style. Finishing the sandwich, I wandered back into the kitchen and pulled a couple more beers out and returned to my seat. Sheldon was taking his own, sweet, time. I hoped that he wasn't doing anything rash back there.

I wandered over to his "collection" and began to peruse the titles. Looking around carefully, I pulled one of the books loose from its perch on the third shelf and flipped it open. Son-of-a-bitch! It was a library book! I dropped it to the floor and began pulling other books out at random! They were all library books! He'd been checking out books and never returning them! There must of been a hundred or so different libraries represented in this "collection"!

"WHAT DO YOU THINK YOU'RE DOING?!"

It was Sheldon. Apparently the falling books had brought him out of his trance, and back to his "reality", such as it was. I turned and faced him, angrily.

"YOU COCK-SUCKING, LIBRARY-LOOTING, PHILISTINE!" I screamed as he stalked towards me. My outburst stunned him, and he stopped dead in his tracks.

"YOU MORALIZING LITTLE WORM! HOW DARE YOU DEPRIVE FUTURE GENERATIONS OF THESE BOOKS, AND, THEN, HAVE THE UNMITIGATED GALL TO LECTURE ME ON 'MAN'S HIGHER MORAL PURPOSE' WHILE YOU STARE UP MY LEG!"

He was silent, for once. No more the strutting peacock, he now stood before me, a broken man.

I picked up the phone and began to dial a number.

"What are you doing?" Sheldon asked.

"I'm calling the library police, and turning you in! There oughta be a fairly substantial reward for all these books!"

"Oh Gawd, please don't do that! I'll pay you handsomely, if you don't turn me in! I don't want to lose my books! Waaaaaaahhhhhh!" He began sobbing, pleading with me as he crossed the floor on his knees. He prostrated himself at my feet, begging. He looked completely pathetic! It was utterly disgusting!

"Hello, Library Police? Yes, I want to turn in someone. What? Yes, I can hold."

As I waited on hold, Sheldon unzipped my fly and pulled out my cock. He popped it into his mouth and began to work on it. Apparently, his skill as a bull-shit artist was not his only talent. He also gave exceptionally good head, for a guy. Yes, Sheldon Van Clam, Esquire, was good; but the money that I would make for turning him in would make it possible for me to retire, start my own poetry magazine and publish my own poetry on a regular basis. Life just got a little better.

* * *

CHERRY

It started out like any other night at "The Hairy Eyeball". That's the coffee bar that I've worked at for the last few years. I started as dishwasher and now I'm the night Manager at this joint. Name's Dusty. Dusty Toole.

Anyway, like I said, it started out like any other night. The house lights were dimmed at 9PM sharp; it was the anal aspect of my nature at work. I was proud of my little place. I liked running it and I liked the people who came in each night.

It was an odd mix of artists, writers, poets, musicians and civilians. Most of the civilians came in for the scene and to be seen with the artists and what-not; while the artists came in to scam on the civilians for the essentials of the bohemi-an lifestyle: money, cigarettes, sex, drugs, food and a forum in which they could puff up their egos.

The writers came in to discuss and argue, mostly argue, about who'd had the rougher life: Celine or Rimbaud, Hemmingway or Lawrence, them or the next guy. It was the same with the poets except they argued more obtusely.

And the musicians were probably the worst. They always wanted "money for nothin' and the chicks for free". And they would argue late into the night about who was the best player of "all" time and who played what the best, etc. Their only saving grace was that they also brought some very beautiful moments into the place.

Like the other night.

The band began to work into the opening number. It was tough and slow work, but they were determined. They knew that their reward was just off-stage in the wings. If they could just find the groove, slip into it and begin to grind away, their beloved Cherry would make her entrance and the change would begin to rain down. So, on they plunged.

They stroked it, they petted it, they teased it and cajoled it. Finally, the groove opened up and something funky began to fill the room. The walls began to pulsate and the crowd began to moan and groan in unison, as if they were watching a trapeze team at the circus.

And then she emerged from behind a velvet curtain. The spotlight operator, caught off guard, bobbled the light and caught her half-way. Her long dresses always perked up the band because, viewed from behind, they always revealed every detail of Cherry's silhouette. She never wore underwear.

Cherry slipped in beside the mic stand, and, grabbing it gingerly, began to moan into the microphone. As she warmed up to the tune that the band was kickin' to death, she also warmed up to the mic stand. She slid her hands up and down that stand as if it was the cock of her dreams. Not since I saw Tina Turner performing at the Shrine Auditorium back in the late sixties, had I seen anyone "do" a mic stand that well.

After making friends with the stand, she now moved up to the mic and began to get acquainted. Cherry's fingers moved over the black shaft like ants discovering an unprotected slice of pie. She pulled the head of the thing up to her lips and nipped it. Somehow, the scraping sound worked within the context of the jam.

Cherry smiled. She knew she could do no wrong tonight. She was in the groove with the band. They were in sync, like lovers, she and the band. The first few songs were like foreplay; they would romp and play, tickle and pet a little; everyone getting "on line".

Then, they'd start "seducing the crowd" (as one of my painter friends was fond of saying). During the next few songs, Cherry, smiling and making eye-contact with the crowd, would begin to work herself into a sweat. Not since the "Divine Miss M", had there been a singer so completely present and vulnerable on stage.

This was always the dicey point in the show; a careless remark from some drunk could throw the whole mood into the crapper. The crowd, mesmerized, would lean forward towards the stage, totally attuned to every nuance of Cherry's performance. The band was positioning themselves for the wild ride that they knew was coming; and Cherry was slowly, gently opening herself like a flower. She deftly peeled back each petal until she could reveal the core, the dripping honey pot. The crowd leaned in closer, as the band worked them, grinding on, twitching out a low, throbbing beat. It was positively PULSATRONIC!

Cherry warbled and cooed, she moaned and groaned. Her hips swayed to the beat. She prowled the edge of the stage, her free hand gliding up and down her dress, the other hand cradling that microphone, using it to caress her cheek, neck, bosom, probing with it and then bringing it back to her lips to howl again, a wounded animal, wounded by the shaft of love's arrow.

The crowd hung on her every sound, her every move. She was the "bouncing ball" and they hypnotically followed her lead. They were the rats to her Pied Piper. They would have followed her to the gates of Hell, no questions asked. But Cherry wasn't that kind of girl. She loved her audience; sometimes one at a time, but mostly as a group. She preferred to lead them to the gates of Heaven, if at all possible.

Tonight, it looked like we were all gonna see God!

The music was beginning to swell, as if the concrete walls of the place might magically bulge out enough to let the excess air escape from the building. The temperature was rising faster than the air-conditioning could deal with it. Beads of sweat began to trickle down the foreheads and temples of the crowd. Bands of sweat were glistening on Cherry's chest and arms and a tiny rivulet was running down her spine and into the crack of her ass, which was flexing and twitching in time to the music. Other parts of Cherry's anatomy were beginning to twitch, as well, but no one except Cherry knew this, except maybe the drummer, who had the most continuous view of her silhouette.

As the musical head began to build, turgidly, Cherry began to go into heat. Her breath came in short, hot gasps. Her eyes closed to slits. She was transforming to another level of being. Her nostrils flared, her nipples stood up so erect, they could have jumped right off her breasts! Her free hand was moving downward, fingers spread apart; the other hand grabbing the head of the mic, pulling it into her chest and up to her lips. A deep moaning sound, that would have made Janis proud, came emanating from her parted lips. She screams, she begs, she pleads with the crowd.

"DON'T STOP!!"

It becomes a chant, a mantra. We all begin to sway, Vipers and Asps, Cobras alike, all being charmed into submission. All ready to merge into a massive, gasping, sweaty heap of throbbing parts and twisted limbs.

Cherry senses this and turns to the band, wild-eyed, ready and willing. She spins like an ice skater, the mic poised above her back-tilted head, her lips parted, tongue extended, as if she intends to deep-throat the damn thing! She plants her feet apart and, bending from the waist, grabs the mic stand to form an odd kind of tripod.

"GIVE IT TO HER!!" Someone yells.

She pauses from her chant and looks at him and smiles. For a fraction of a second, everyone catches a breath; and then the band slams it home.

Cherry rises on her toes, rocking, but she takes everything the band can give and still she chants on. It's positively Bolero-esque! It's a revival meeting gone hallelujah-fucking insane! It's frenzy. It's what scared the Moral Majority and Tipper Gore and every flag waving politico from here right back to the birth of Rock & Roll!

It was group sex without any latex or fear of deadly disease. It was the primal, fucking, Bim, Bam, Boom of life!

"DON'T STOP!!!"

Cherry stood up, rose up really, ascended to an almost vertical position. Every eye in the room was on her. Even blind Pete was lookin' in her direction. I didn't know how much more of this action the place could stand. A faintly, boney smell was rising from the crowd, telling me that Cherry wasn't the only one getting off tonight.

But the band was taking us all on a long, sweaty, horsefuckin' ride and there was nothing anyone could do about it. They were giving it to Cherry with an intensity that would have exhausted most; but she took it and, though she was close to a hyper-ventilation induced blackout, was giving everyone a run for their money.

I, along with every other male (and probably a few females too) in the room, wanted her. I could imagine her crouched over me, riding me like the hounds of Hell were nipping at our heals. I could almost feel her sweaty ass grinding against my crotch; her breasts pressed into my chest; my fingers, like blue flames, licking up and down her back; grabbing the cheeks of her ass as I drove into her, churning away; and all the while, her lips so close to mine, muttering a litany of:

"DON'T STOP!!!"

The band had reached a fevered pitch. The finale was fast approaching. Cherry looked at me, thru me, knowing that I wanted to take her, would take her if given half a chance. She smiled. And then, as if she had been shot with ten thousand volts, she collapsed to her knees, convulsing, wave upon wave. The melody of the tune surged and receded, plummeted and soared; the various instruments rising in a cacophonous euphoria which then peeled off, one by one, into a staccato-like bass and drum solo. Cherry was pleading in a whisper, but the band just didn't have much more to give her. They'd wrung out just about every note possible. Now they were ready for a cigarette and a towel.

Still she wanted more. Staggering back to her feet, Cherry straddled the mic stand and began to slide up and down, up and down. The bass player, a big sweating mountain of a man took a big breath, as if he was hitting on some prime bud, and began to slap out a funk beat; a bone-dislocating, organ-pulverizing, pulsatronic beat; the kind of a beat that could disrupt one's atomic assembly.

Cherry moaned into the mic, and slid a little faster. Would she really cum? Could she really let herself go in front of this crowd? Or wouldn't that cheapen the moment.

"D O N ' T   S T O P ! ! ?"

Mercifully, the bass player ran out of steam. The whole band came to a halt and for one brief moment, we were ALL ONE! We'd all gotten there at the same time! It was a moment to be savored and we did savor it. All, except Cherry.

Cherry stood limply at the mic. She was panting. I thought I saw a tear run down her cheek, but it could have been a bead of sweat, too. She'd gotten the entire room off, but she still wasn't satisfied! She just stood there, glazed, not believing that it was over. Someone handed her a bottle of wine and she took a big swig. This brought her back down to earth. She headed for the back door.

Outside, as she French-inhaled a cigarette, Cherry leaned up against the cool, plaster wall and watched a cloud slide under the moon. A light breeze cooled the moist film of sweat on her arms and neck and tickled the throbbing place. She smiled to herself and let the wind finish her off.

*   *   *

COCK FIGHT

I remember many years back, I got into a really, good, brawl. I was working the door at this coffee place, back in the early nineties (you know, back when all that chi-chi coffee bullshit was popular; everyone was *soooo* European!). Maybe you heard of it? You know, <u>The Hairy Eyeball</u>. No? Well, whatever!

Well, anyway, as I said, I was working the door and these two guys come in with three or four broads draped over their arms and the one guy says to me, "whataya mean I got to pay to come in here, we ain't still in Vegas are we? Ha!"

At this point, as if on cue, his whole party laughs. As one.

I'm thinkin' that this guy's got a lot of juice with somebody important. He's either a big fish or someone who thinks he is, and now he's gonna piss on the peon doorman just to show his pal and their dates how big a man he really is.

"Well, hell, Bub, what'er we paying for? What's this dump got that's so freakin' special that it's worth my hard earned money? What are you lookin' at, pal?"

His girlfriend was showing me her I.D. She wasn't a natural blonde. Interesting. I wondered what else was fake.

Huh?

Oh, sorry. The fat motherfucker was leaning over (as far as he could) and staring into my face. So, I explained, for the thousandth time, that the band was on a break and they'd have t' pay if they stayed inside, but if they went outside there was no charge. Or they could stay and if they didn't like the band and left within a half hour, I'd refund their money.

"Oh Harry, what the fuck, let's stay for awhile. Besides, we need to sober up a little for the drive back to the Hotel California."

It was the "blonde". I thought, man, these morons are staying in a high class joint like the California? Shit! I hope this guy, Harry, don't decide to fuck with me!

But luck was with me, still. Harry relented and produced a wad of bills the size of my fist. I noticed a pinkie ring with the initials "HRH" in, what looked like, diamonds. Subtle. He peeled off a Cee-note and handed it to me.

"Shit man! I can't break that! It'll take all my change! You got anything smaller?"

"That's what all my girlfriends say! Haw ha!"

Again they all laugh. Pathetic.

"Sorry there partner, but it's that or nothing!"

"Here, Harry, let me get that for you. You can figure out a way to pay me back later."

Harry's gal was payin' me as she stared into his Foster Grants. They weaved on in and headed for the cappuccino line. Geezus! Maybe, they were lawyers! Yeah, that's probably it, they're lawyers.

I watched Harry's girlfriend wobble along behind the pack, her dress accentuating her sleek waist and her magnificent ass! I thought about that little slice of heavenly pie that was hidden up inside there. Then, I thought about how ol' Harry would be having a late night snack, in a few hours; while I would be sweeping sidewalks and putting up the chairs. Keyrist! I hated lawyers.

More people came in. The band came back on and started puttin' a move on the crowd. They were good at that. The lead singer was double jointed, and all the joints in the room were doubling, including mine.

Soon I had forgotten about Harry. The night was lookin' better and better.

As the band was takin' it's second break, Harry and company filed past.

"We didn't like the band and we want our money back."

Whaaat?

Harry leaned over again. I could hear the sound of creaking leather, like maybe he had on a truss? I wouldn't be surprised, the gut on this asshole was big enough to use as a mooring buoy out in the harbor. Harry's breath had that mix of stale alcohol, cigars and burnt coffee. It was a delightful bouquet. For "Blondie's" sake, I hoped he brushed when they got back to their room.

"Listen, you little nobody. Do you know who used to own this ring, before I had it removed as partial payment on a debt?"

He was waving the pinkie ring in my face.

"H.R. Halderman! You *do* know who that is, don't you?"

I looked at the ring and then at his face, then my face, reflected in his glasses, then back at the ring. "Yeah, I know who he is. But I know that you're no Dick Nixon!" And then I got pissed off.

"Listen, you mother, I told you how it was gonna be if you came in here! I was a nice guy about it. I coulda refused to let you in here, cause you're drunk, but, NOOOO! I let you in. And now you wanta get your money back after being in HERE FOR ONE AND A HALF FREAKIN' HOURS?!"

"Harry, let's go. Leave it alone. We've had our fun. Let's go, baby, please?"

"Well, okay. But let me give you a little advice, son. Be nicer to the public, they're always right, Heh heh heh."

And just to prove that he was immune, Mr. John Q. Public, reached over and tweaked my nose, good and hard. Then, he was gone, laughing with his cronies, as they headed down the hill to their car. I sat there rubbing my nose. I wanted to chase after them, but fear of losing my job, as well as my life, loomed large in my mind's eye.

Later that night, after work, I went down to the Rusty Gullet; a refined, drinking establishment just down the street (on the way to the Hotel California) where it was always summertime and the livin' was easy!

I was regaling the doorman with the story of Harry and company when, from the other end of the bar, a great cry rang out. Every eye in the place (except old Blind Ted's) turned towards the voice.

"YOU ARE FREAKIN' DEAD!" It was Harry. Harry appeared to be very mad at someone in the "Rec Room" where the pool tables were. "Come here, you little CUNT!"

The bar was stone, cold silent. I've never heard it so quiet in there, except during the day. Even the music box had stopped. It was like we were suspended in time, like someone had sprayed the air with "Roofy" mist. A strange, hypnotic reverie scooped me up and carried me towards the back room.

A shrieking scream pierced the air and broke me free. The world seemed to shatter above me, but it was merely a bottle exploding nearby.

"OOOOOOWWWWWW MY GAAAAAAAWWWWWWWD, HE"S GOT A KNIFE!!!!!!!" Someone screamed. I think it was the bartender's mother. She pack's a mean uppercut; learned it when she was a Green Beret (before they found out she was a woman, and sent her home in secret; what an embarrassment for Duke and the boys).

Next thing I know, the whole bar's pouring into the back room to see what's going on. Unfortunately, I'm ahead of the pack, so I get jammed into the room, ending up pressed against the pool table next to Harry's blonde friend. Harry looks at me, doesn't recognize me (thank you Geezus!), and moves towards her, unsteadily.

There's blood on his lapel and on the side of his head. Someone's cold-cocked the motherfucker with a beer bottle and all's it's done is *really* piss him off!

The pinkie ring flashes as he approaches, menacingly waving the knife back and forth, like the tail of an irritated cat. And then it happens.

He recognizes me.

"YOU!"

Oh. Shit.

I don't know what came over me. I moved like I was possessed by ninja samurai! I've never studied any martial arts, except Tai Chi Chuan (and that was years ago). Hell! I'm a lover not a fighter! And I'm not much of a lover, for that matter. But here I am, grabbing a pool cue and the "bridge" from the rack behind me and, in one, fluid motion; I'm spinning towards Harry like Bruce-freakin'-Lee!

He lunges towards me; I parry and thrust, using the "bridge" to knock the knife loose. It falls to the table, harmlessly. Then, I'm using the cue like a lance, thrusting it deep into Harry's mid-section. It's like impaling a marshmallow on the end of a coat hanger. Harry exhales loudly, his arms wind-milling without much success. He is beginning to stagger backwards. The bartender is warming up her "haymaker". I push Harry around and into her, using the "bridge" like a fly swatter. The crowd leans in, the melee is about to begin. I'm afraid it won't go well for Harry, tonight. There is a rustling of pool cues behind me. I grab the fake blonde and dive under the pool table with her. We scramble out the other side and make it out the back door.

In the alley, leaning up against the wall, catching our breaths and assessing the damage, we both stare in amazement back into the doorway. Inside, the mob seems to be playing tug-of-war with Harry. It reminds me of a tango; a slow, deadly tango.

Oh what a tangoed web we weave!

I cringe as the sound of fists thudding against flesh drifts out to us. Harry isn't going to be real happy about all this when he wakes up in the morning. I turn to the blonde and ask her if she can drive. She says yes and staggers off down the alley.

Within a few minutes, she pulls up and double parks it, with the motor still running.

"What are you going to do?"

"I'm waitin' for the cops to show up. When they do, it'll be a stampede comin' out of that doorway. That's when we'll grab Harry and toss what's left of him into the back seat."

Just as I finish explaining it to her, several guys come stumbling out of the door.

"OOOOHHH SHIT! IT'S THE COPS!"

Pandemonium breaks out. People are scrambling over each other to get out the door. A woman screams. Something crashes and breaks. Harry appears in the doorway, sticking there for a moment like a blood clot, then bursting out into the alley followed by the remaining crowd. They scatter down the alley, like birds suddenly released from the cage, whooping and shouting.

In a few moments, it's quiet again, except for the purring motor and the groaning lump of lard with the pinkie ring.

We grab him at bow and stern, but he's too heavy. So, we get him under the arms and drag him to the car. Rolling him over onto his knees, we get him halfway in. I run around to the other side and pull him onto the back seat, while "blondie" leans over and lifts him by the belt. I wonder where the rest of the party is, we could sure use their help, about now. Of course, I wouldn't be getting such a swell view down the front of her dress, but, hey!

"Are you going to need a hand with this ASSHOLE?"

"Well, thanks, but I'm sure Harry won't mind sleepin' it off in the car tonight.

But let me give you a little reward for standin' up for me in there. Thank you."

She planted a wet one on me. Her tongue slid into my mouth and began to do loop-the-loops with mine. I planted my hands on her ass and began to knead the cheeks together, like I was trying to make one, single buttock. I leaned into her, my erection pressing against her belly. She groaned for a moment and then disengaged.

"I'd better be going." she breathed, hoarsely, as she got in behind the wheel. "I've got to catch an early flight to Frisco. Here, call me, okay?"

I looked at the card that she had handed me as she drove off towards the sunrise. I put it in my pocket next to the pinkie ring. As I turned to head up the alley, I noticed something lying on the ground. It was Harry's wad of bills. Picking it up, I unfolded the roll. It was as I had suspected, mostly small change, singles and the like; but there were four hundreds, about ten fifties and so on. It was a good haul by my standards. Enough to last a few months, if I played it close to the margin!

I stopped in at the "Good Fairy's" to celebrate.

"To Harry!" I said, after buying a round for the assembled losers. We drank our beers "Bukowski-style" and I went home and dreamed about that kiss.

* * *

CARL

"Aw, you ain't got shit for brains!"

"I'm telling you, it's the gawdamn'd Mexicans! Them and that gawdamned Clitton and his gawdamned NASDAK!"

Carl thought that he had heard it all. He'd been working the bars on Waterfront Way here in the Harbor Gateway for close to five years and he'd heard stories that could make Mike Tyson break down and cry like a baby. He'd heard some of the biggest lies ever told, tales so tall, the shuttle Columbia would have to make a course adjustment to avoid a mid-space collision with them. But tonight, tonight even Carl was impressed by the audacity and truly bone-headed pretzel logic that the two old boys at the end of the bar were spouting.

These two worked up in Chino on one of those worm spreads. It was a wiggly job at best. Carl always wondered what it was like driving a herd of worms to the railhead so's they could be shipped to anglers everywhere. He'd heard about the annual wormdrive for three years running. He'd always wanted to go. The tantalizing smell of a mesquite barbecue, a Jackalope turning on a spit, while off in the distance, the gentle rustling of a million worms being hosed down by some fella with a water truck and a C# harmonica with a couple of bad notes. Carl's reverie did not last long.

"What are you talkin' about ya old fool? The pres'dent would never do any-thing to us, he needs us. Think about it...he's a fisherman! He needs us for our *worms!* How do ya figure it's the Mex?"

"I'll tell ya. Remember old man Jones?"

"The one who still has the first two cents he ever stole?! Haw haw haw!"

"Yeah...off the eyes of his grandmother! Awhooo!"

They both nearly fell off their stools with laughter. Carl hated their guts.

Maybe he's slip them a Mickey Finn and feed them to Lola. Then he'd dump whatever was left of them in a worm trough near Bakersfield. Carl daydreamed on as he wiped a shot glass clean.

"Yeah, well remember how he had that old pickup for sale?"

"The one with that big old dent in the fender?"

"From running into that old lady over at the Super K Mart?"

"That's 'er! How long has he had that thing for sale?"

Claudio Parentela

"She-it, why it's been at least three years!"

"And hasn't the price on that gawdamned truck been droppin' steadily?"

"Ever since the Prez stopped blowin' that sax and started blowin' his job! Har har har!"

"Well, I figured it out today when I went over there to try and talk him down a little bit more. See I been workin' on him for about six months now and I almost got him down to where he'd end up payin' me to take the damned thing off'n his hands! Maybe even get him to throw in a couple of nights with his pretty young wife, too!"

"Aw shit, she's a looker!"

Carl had seen the "looker". She was as attractive as the grill of a Peterbuilt COE after a late August run to Tonopah!

"So, I went over ta his place with two hundred dollars in my pocket and what do I see? Two guys in tight jeans, pointy-toed boots and ka-boy hats a'comin' away from his porch! I look't over ta old man Jones and he was busy makin hissef a *new sign*!"

"What?!"

"Yeah! Yuh coulda knocked me down with a wormfart!"

"A new sign? What fer?"

"What fer? Why them Mex's made him an offer that was close ta three times what he was askin'!"

"Gawdy!"

"Yeah! Them bean jockey's must be poolin' their welfare and paychecks, cause they got all the high priced jobs sewn up! Hell, they act like they was here before we was! It just ain't right!"

They fingered their empty glasses for a minute in silence.

"Three times?!"

"I know whatcha mean! Hey Carl!? How's about another round here, for a couple of Americans!"

Carl moved towards them. The blood of Aztecs throbbed in his veins. He hoped Lola would appreciate his gesture. It had been days since her last feeding and he knew she'd be hungry.

* * *

Two Drink Minimum

"Cock sucking son of a bitch! You MISERABLE piece of goddamned cock sucking piece of shit!"

Across the room from me, Bob yelled for about the two hundredth time. It was eleven AM and he'd already had at least one beer. You see a lot of that in the trades. Lots of guys don't really get off the ground until they've had their morning pull. But most of those guys aren't ready to kill a piece of drywall because it could only behave like a piece of drywall, either.

Not so with Bob. He was ready to open up a big ol' can of whoopass on that piece of wallboard and was reaching for his trusty framing hammer.

"It needs a minor adjustment," he said, with just a hint of malice.

I thought the next words out of his mouth would be "It started it!" But was wrong when he screamed *cock sucking son of a bitch, miserable piece of goddamned cock sucking piece of shit!*

"Two hundred and one," I thought to myself.

"Am I doing this right?"

This, from my co-worker Helen, who was a cute in a sort of psychotically imbalanced and high maintenance way – in that way that bad girls get when they've been bad too long; like Britney, the Pop icon...bad and slutty one minute and virginal and pissed off, the next. Like that.

Helen was scraping the wall a few feet to my left. She was working real hard; it was important to her that she do it right. I think she was trying to prove something to our boss...like the fact that she needed her job and he really could start trusting her again.

I watched her working. She was really tearing into her job. I looked at her form, the way she leaned into each stroke, the way her arms tightened up as she pulled back, her determined look as she focused on each new section...and yes, the way her tits bobbed. She had on the loosest undershirt I have ever seen. And every time she leaned over, there they were, on view for anyone interested. The guy across the way had made their acquaintance earlier and I'm sure, like me, he was wondering how long it would take before he made his move. I knew I had to make a sacrifice. I knew what I must do next.

"That looks fine, Helen, you're really giving it what for."

"Cock sucking son of a bitch! You miserable piece of godamned cock sucking piece of shit!"

"But I have to say that that shirt is giving me a problem."

"What? My shirt? What's wrong with my goddamned shirt?"

Oh boy.

"There's nothing wrong with your shirt except that it shows off your tits every time you bend over."

"What??? You're looking at my tits? Is that what you are saying? You..."

"Cock sucking son of a bitch!"

I had to turn away from her, for some reason this was suddenly very funny. It was like a Monty Python skit. I imagined myself in the Office of Bad Chemistry, being abused by John Clease. I hate to admit it but I was starting to enjoy this banter. Between the two of them it was quite a circus. Helen on one side firing the standard line of bullshit, laced with a healthy dose sexual innuendo and drug chatter; and Bob on the other devoting half the day to his new mantra, punctuating it with short protests of "aw, come on.." or "that's it baby, that's it..." It was a three ring circus. "Where the hell is *my* ring?" I wondered.

In construction work, it's not just the steelworkers who use crude language. In fact, these days you hear about people saying shit that they shouldn't all the time. It's a fact when you put men and women in the same room, someone's bound to get ideas or, worse, frisky. Helen and I traded smart-assed comments most of the day before. Yet, buried in all that, Helen also told me a lot about herself (I've learned to take notes when the cute –but dangerous– chicks begin to drop innocent, little clues about why you should give them, at least, an extra car length of room). She was a real 'chatty Cathy', turns out. I soon realized that there was no way in hell that trying to get beyond her come-ons (and into her pants) was worth all the subsequent grief I would have to endure after we caught our breaths. I hated to give up the peep show, but it was just gonna make this...

"Cock sucking son of a bitch, miserable piece of goddamned cock sucking piece of shit!"

...job that much harder to endure. And I had to endure it as long as I could because, like Helen, I needed the money. And unlike Helen, well more specifically, Helen's tits, I wasn't going to be able to sweet-talk the boss, if push came to shove. We both knew it; both knew she had the edge.

"So, you think it's my fault, you're a perve?"

Ah, the trump card!

"Hey, you don't care if we see your tits every time you bend over? Well, shit girl, take the damned thing off!" No sense in beating around the bush, I always say.

"Fuck you! There's nothing wrong with my shirt."

She was inspecting her shirt. She was right, when she stood up it was a nice, respectably loose shirt. But when she leaned over again, there they were, again. And I'd think "Hello girls!" This went on until Bob swore again and she stopped scraping and stood up very close to me, saying "I guess you're right, what do you think I should do about it? It's not like my tits are big enough to be a problem..."

"Your tits are just fine..." What was I saying? I sure didn't mind looking at them, but I knew that trouble was a'brewing because I was starting to think more about her tits than I was about the job at hand. So I had to either get her to cover up or just blow off the job and try and do her during lunch.

"How about putting on another shirt, weren't you wearing one earlier this morning?"

She looked at me and smiled and for a moment I was twenty years back in time in Hermosa Beach with my hands up Crazy Jane's shirt... And just like then, I watched as the shadows flickered across her eyes and I *knew* there was something way out of whack with her. In Crazy Jane's case, she was about to be labeled "certifiable." In Helen's case, I wasn't quite sure how close she was to the edge, but I knew that I didn't want to get sucked in (even "on" was losing it's appeal). Except for the tits. They presented their case very well. Come to think of it, so did Crazy Jane's.

"Oh. Okay."

And like that she headed for the bathroom. Simple. Easy. A done deal. I went back to addressing the wall. I had to make it flat and there was a sizable indentation in it.

"Cock sucking son of a bitch, miserable piece of goddamned cock sucking piece of shit!"

I had to agree. Whoever built this apartment slash condo complex was either in a really big hurry or a complete moron. Come to think of it, they were probably both (I seem to recall there was some big scandal back in the early seventies when these things were built).

Helen came out of the bathroom. "I figured out what the problem was...it was my hair-do."

Hair-do? I looked over at her. She'd put it up in a bun of sorts. She came over to her spot on the wall and bent over to start scraping. "There, isn't that nicer?" She asked.

She was happy, her tits were happy. Who was I to upset the apple cart?

"Yeah, you're right, *that* was the problem. Yes sirree..."

"Cock sucking son of a bitch, miserable piece of goddamned cock sucking piece of shit!"

Geezus! I thought to myself, this guy is really starting to get to me. *But I should be able to get through this, I'm a fucking adult, right? I know what's what.*

Something came crashing across the room and bounced off the wall next to me. I turned around just in time to see a tape measure go skidding across the floor.

"Hey, you crazy motherfucker, knock that shit off!" I yelled over at him, looking at Helen who winced and bent over even farther.

"What'd you say?" Bob was turning towards me, slowly like he was going to say DRAW! next and whip out a hogleg the size of a canon. I'd managed to hit the 'whoopass' button on him and I could see it was gonna get ugly.

"I said, you crazy motherfucker, throwing your tools around like you were the only one in here. Get a fuckin' grip, man, it's embarrassing to listen to you.

You're a man, act like one!"

Bob looked at me. Really, he gaped at me, mouth slightly ajar, as if he'd never heard this before and was now cut to the quick. I noticed he was missing a front tooth. *Why doesn't he have a lisp,* I wondered to myself?

"Did you call me...crazy? I'm not crazy, man, it ain't right to say that, man, it just ain't right. Cock sucking son of a bitch..." he muttered, his voice trailing off.

"Well, shit man, what am I supposed to think, when *you're* the one coming unglued, throwing your shit around? Is this what you call sane?"

Bob looked at me like he'd just been called to the Mother Superior's office for cussing. "It ain't right," he muttered under his breath, "you cock sucking son of a bitch, miserable piece of goddamned cock sucking piece of shit!" Then he turned around and began to use the hammer to punch holes in the wall. The wall put up a fight, but was no match for the hammer. Bob didn't care. He droned, "cock sucking son of a bitch, miserable piece of goddamned cock sucking piece of shit," muttering it low about every other hammer swing.

Whomp! Whomp!

"Cock sucking son of a bitch, miserable piece of goddamned cock sucking piece of shit!"

Whomp! Whomp!

"You cock sucking son of a bitch, miserable piece of goddamned cock sucking piece of shit!"

And so on.

It was like a cross between Queen's "We Will Rock You" and Pink Floyd's "Money" (just the opening). I found myself smiling. The humor was fleeting. As the mantra continued, old Bob began to get more excited. Pretty soon the whomping was replaced with a crashing sound as Bob threw the hammer down, shattering a tile at his feet. He spun around to face the room and began to say, very, very slowly, like James Cagney might say in an old movie, you know, right before he pumps a shot or two into George Raft:

"YOU...DIRTY...MOTHERFUCKING...COCK SUCKING... SON OF A...BITCH!"

This was followed by a slow burn. I was surprised that Bob could do a slow-burn since he was such a hot-head...but there it was. You could almost imagine the steam coming out of his ears as he continued:

"MISERABLE...PIECE OF...GODAMNED... COCK SUCKING... PIECE... OF... SHIT!"

This last part, was said with such vehemence, I half expected blood to shoot out of his eyes, or things to start exploding around me, like in a bad Stephen King movie.

"Bob, honey? Can I do something to help?" It was Helen. It was a girlish voice. I looked at her. Her tits were not girlish, but her current personality was. It was unsettling. Another 'red flag.' So all that banter about her fucked up marriage was true. I was pretty sure that her childhood wasn't that uneventful either. She had the whole slut/saint/wounded deer thing wired. It had served her well over the years. She was 'daddy's girl' and working it quite well. I had already started calling her 'Princess.'

Like me, Bob was looking at her tits, mesmerized really. "You can have 'em," I thought and went back to work. I heard him say to her, over my shoulder, "Well, yeah, Helen, there is this one thing you can do for me..."

Here it comes...

"...you could come over here and scrape this wall for me and..." It trailed off. I heard her move over there. They started to talk, or so I thought, but it was just their slowly escalating mantras of "cock sucking son of a bitch, miserable piece of goddamned cock sucking piece of shit" and "there's nothing wrong with my shirt."

I was making some progress on the wall. It was looking like it might work out okay. Bob had settled down. I guess Helen's breasts had soothed the savage beast (or however that saying goes). She came back over to 'our' wall and began to scrape. It was good to see her and her friends again. The world was right at last. Even the radio, which had been blaring out 'speed-metal' (the industry standard, when it comes to demolition) most of the morning, was playing some sentimental rock ballad. I sighed. It was good to be here, now.

Suddenly my reverie was broken by Bob's overly dramatic rendition of the chorus. He was really getting into it. Of course, he couldn't sing for shit. In fact, there wasn't a bucket made that was big enough for him to carry this tune in!

"Well at least he's not yelling." I thought.

Ah, innocence.

"Cock sucking son of a bitch, miserable piece of goddamned cock sucking piece of shit!"

I'd had it. Screw the cautious-I'm-not-gonna-come-down-to-his-level approach.

"Bob? Why don't you shut the fuck up?"

"Cock sucking son of a...what'dya just say?" Bob turned slowly. He had this vein on his forehead that looked like it was two beats away from exploding. "What did you say?" He asked again.

"Oh shit, now you've done it." Helen said cringing lower to the floor. She was probably right. But even a mature adult like me could only take so much.

Bob was back to muttering under his breath, "that just ain't right, telling me to shut the fuck up...cock sucking, son of a..."

"Bob? You got another beer? You better take a break right now."

I watched him warily, while he moved across the room and out onto the balcony, where his beer stash was. He lit a cigarette and opened a beer. I waited. I knew that the shit was drifting towards the fan, that soon he'd be ready to defend his 'honor'. Bob finished his smoke and slammed the remains of the beer. He turned to face me.

I looked at my watch. It was almost one o'clock, just in time for the matinee.

"All right, motherfucker, let's git to it."

*   *   *

THE GIFT

Harry sat quietly in the waiting room. A copy of Field and Stream lay open on his lap, but the article on fly fishing held no interest for him. The magazine was more a prop than anything else; a reason for him to stare downward, to avoid looking into the eyes of the other patients. The room was full of conversation, but Harry didn't join in, since the voices he heard were in his head. It was too hard to distinguish between the real voices and the thought voices. Harry had learned early on that it was best not to attract attention to himself by announcing this special talent of his. But, lately it had become the curse of his days and nights.

There was a time when Harry could control the voices by not making eye contact with the person in question. Then he just had to live with a constant murmuring, a kind of oscillating whirring sound that modulated between louder and softer tones. When the Beatles came out with Revolution Number Nine on the White album, Harry was elated. He mistakenly assumed that someone else heard what he did and had been able to reproduce it! Unfortunately, this wasn't the case. George Harrison would reveal in his autobiography, years later, that the #9 track was actually an attempt to communicate with the spirit world and reach John's aunt Julia; astral projection and that whole magical mystery thing — it was back in the day when we were all a little more open.

Now the millennium was closing in, as were the walls and Harry was visiting the county shrink. He'd been experiencing uncontrollable bouts of fear that would paralyze him and leave him trying to scream; only nothing would come out. He'd find himself screaming at the top of his lungs, only nothing would be audible. But in his mind, his screams would drown out the other voices. This was great, except that he was getting a lot of funny looks from people; imagine a guy standing in a lobby doing the silent scream bit. It was pretty disconcerting. Harry had been asked to leave or physically escorted from quite a few places. It was getting so he couldn't go to the store to buy groceries or underwear. He had to eat. And change his shorts.

The hardest part about the gift was sitting calmly in the same room with other people and their thoughts. The guy across the room from him looked like a banker, very respectable and all, but he was day dreaming about fondling his daughter. Harry felt another scream coming on. He tried to tune out this guy's thinking, knowing that it would make him nauseous to be privy to all the ugly details, but there's a certain sick fascination with the gory details. Just ask anyone who's slowed down at an accident, just in case they might get to see something. It's human nature to want to sneak a look, ask Lot's wife.

Sitting between Harry and this other guy was a woman in her late thirties, although it's kinda hard to tell because she's obviously been through quite a hard life. Harry's seen her before, around town. He glances at her face for just a second and hears her screaming silently too. She's just found out that she has AIDS. Fear is pounding her like the storm surge before hurricane Andrew. Fear is burying her like a slag heap collapsing on po' folk in a West Virginia mining slum. She is screaming and screaming. Harry screams with her.

As they sit silently, screaming , the receptionist opens her little, glass window. The screaming stops. It is replaced with anticipation.

"Mr. Harry Smithers? The Doctor will see you now." The receptionist is warm and friendly. But Harry knows otherwise. She feels vastly superior to the peons that she sees waiting everyday to be cured by the DOCTOR. She is frustrated, an ass kissing sycophant who is totally smitten with the Doctor. She wants him, bad. But the Doc's interests lay in another direction and he has shown no interest in her. Her obsession is slowly turning her into a certifiable man-hating megalomaniac. One day, in the not so distant future, Harry will read about her in the paper. It won't be a happy story.

"Sit down Mr. Smithers;" the Doctor's tone is reassuring. "Now what seems to be the problem?"

Harry doesn't look the Doc in the eye. He knows better. He knows not to play his trump card too soon.

"Doc, I've got this little problem;" Harry begins, slowly, knowing that he's got to play the Doc like a fish, set the hook, play him and reel him in; "I hear voices all the time."

The Doctor leans forward over his desk. At first, he was sitting with arms up, hands folded behind his head. Now, he is leaning forward, his hands under his desk, fumbling with the syringe loaded with tranquilizer that he keeps for emergencies like this one. Harry makes a mental note of this.

"Tell me, Harry, you don't mind if I call you Harry, do you?"

"Naw, go ahead, Doc."

"Fine. So, Harry, when do you hear these voices?"

"All the time Doc, all the time."

"Even now?"

"Yeah."

"Are they telling you to do anything?"

"No, not really."

"What do you mean, 'not really'?"

It was time to set the hook. "I mean that the voices aren't talking to me, per se, they're kinda just always there and I can hear them, but I don't really listen to them very much, except lately."

Harry looked at the Doctor. The Doctor was thinking about what Harry was saying but he was also thinking about his dry cleaning and his mother's birthday, which he'd forgotten, and renewing his NAMBLA dues and...Harry knew he was losing the Doctor's interest. It was time to play the trump card.

"Don't worry Doc, your dry cleaning is gonna be fine."

The Doc looked at him quizzically. "My dry cleaning?"

"Yeah. And your mom won't mind another late birthday card, either."

"How did you know about that?" The Doctor asks, trying hard not to think about NAMBLA.

"I told you, I hear voices, but it's really more like I can hear your thoughts;" Harry replied. He could see that the Doctor was almost convinced. So he dropped the last bomb.

"Man-Boy love."

"Wha, what?!"

"You heard me." Harry was looking right through the Doctor when he said this. The Doctor twitched, like a delicate butterfly that Harry had just pinned into his collection.

"By the way, your secretary won't wait much longer for you to return her advances;" Harry continued; "She's gonna cut you down to size!" Harry was trying to be diplomatic.

"Are you threatening me?!" The Doctor said, trying not to let on how disconcerted this was making him.

"No, Doc. This is fact not fiction!"

"So, what's the problem? It seems to me that if I could read people's minds, I'd want to use it to my advantage!"

Harry leaned back in his chair and began his story.

"It's not that bad being able to hear people's thoughts. Most of the time I don't mind. But sometimes I hear some really horrendous thoughts and it makes me want to cry, to see such sadness and pain in the world.

"Sadness and pain is a part of life, Harry. The world is not a very wonderful place these days."

"Yeah, but Doc, you don't seem to understand. All the things that people are thinking, I can hear."

"All?" Harry knew that he'd be skeptical.

"Yes, all. Don't believe me? Test me. You'll see."

"Is this like clairvoyance? Can you see the future?"

"In as much as someone's thoughts can reveal what they will be doing next." Harry said.

"What was it that you said earlier about my secretary?" Harry knew that the Doctor was going to fire her and this was going to be his excuse.

"I said that she's got the hots for you and that she's getting tired of waiting for you to come-on to her. Real tired! I think she'll try something tonight before you leave the office."

"Hm. That's very interesting. I think I know how to test you."

The Doctor took Harry into a room next to his office and put a headset on him. It had a little microphone like a receptionist would wear and an earpiece. The doctor explained that he was going back into his office and call in his receptionist, using some excuse, to quiz her. Harry was to read her thoughts and relay them to him by speaking into the microphone. The Doctor would hear him through a tiny earpiece that he would be wearing, as well. Harry sat down and concentrated on the Doctor's thoughts. He had to tune out the other voices in the immediate area. The Doctor left him and went into the other room. He thought about his NAMBLA dues again when a voice came over the earpiece.

"Doc, that's sick! Why don't you take up another hobby?"

The Doctor winced and called in the receptionist.

"Miss Barnes, could you come in here for a second?"

"Yes, Doctor? Why, where's Mr. Smithers?" Miss Barnes asked.

"Oh, I sent him down the hall to the restroom. Tell me Miss Barnes, say what is your first name, anyway?"

Janice is surprised that you are even curious. She's getting excited.

"My name is Janice."

"Janice? What a lovely name. Janice, it's come to my attention that you're not very happy working for me, is this true? By the way, that's a very attractive uniform you've got on; I like the way it reveals just a little bit, but not too much, of your womanly charms."

Now she's really confused. She wants you but she's also wondering who's been talking behind her back.

"Janice, it doesn't matter who's been talking. Let's just say a little bird told me, and leave it at that. Now, as to the truth of the matter, I understand that you'd like to get even for being ignored all these months, but I assure you that there is little you could do to peak my interests."

"Oh, now Doctor, are you sure?" Janice had moved around the desk and positioned herself on the edge so that the Doctor couldn't help but see up her dress. She was also grabbing the gold letter opener, which lay on the desk.

Watch it Doc, if you don't respond correctly, she's gonna stab you with your letter opener. She wants you to take her right there on the desk, but she also wants to prune your ego and I think you know what I mean.

"Now, Janice, not only would it be inappropriate for me to make love to you here, it would be unfair to my wife and my career. Besides, you don't really think that I could be moved by the vision of your thigh, do you. I'm a trained professional, after all."

Janice opened her legs and unhooked the bottom two buttons on her dress uniform. It was evident that she did not wear panties.

"Are you sure that this doesn't effect you, somehow? I could do such

things to you. Forget your wife, that frigid hag! Forget those boys, forget all that you have known and let me prove to you my desire!"

And so saying, she pulled the Doctor's head into her bosom, with one hand, while she positioned the letter opener with the other.

Careful Doc, she's got that dagger ready. She's struggling with the strength of her desires. She's not sure if she wants you alive or dead.

"Janice please! What do you think you're doing? I'm your superior! My God!"

She's noticed that you've got an erection. She wants it. Doc, you'd better give it to her before she decides to take it.

"Don't feed me that ethics bullshit, Doc! I see that hard-on in your pants. I'm gonna get it, one way or the other!" And so saying, Janice produced the letter opener, brandishing it menacingly.

The doctor backed away from his desk, covering his crotch with his hand while searching for something to fend her off. There was nothing within his grasp and she soon had him up against the wall, the knife pressed flat against his cheek as she leaned into him. The Doc looked scared. Harry could read his thoughts too. He was begging Harry to help him out of this dilemma. Harry would respond, but, first he wanted the Doc to sweat a little bit. He needed a taste of retribution. Harry knew it would be humbling.

Janice pressed herself into him. She could feel his hard-on through his pants. She ground her hips into him. Leaning very close to his ear, she said; "Let's face it, Doc, I know you want some of this, don't you?" Then she pulled his hand and thrust it between her legs. The Doc flinched as he felt her moistness. He struggled to escape her grasp but she was a lot stronger than he had suspected. And she had a knife, which she was using to trace the outline of his Adam's Apple.

"Give me what I want, or else I'll have to *take it!*" These last words were emphasized by her grabbing hold of him. The Doc's thoughts were plain as day.

Help me?!

Harry started to move towards the door. Just as he reached for the handle, he 'heard' the Doc's next thought: *Oh, Janice!*

He opened the door a crack and peered out. The Doc was still scared but there was something new on his mind. Harry watched the two of them going at it. The Doc was a straight arrow after all.

Later, after it was over and the Doc had cleaned up and regained his composure, Harry re-entered the office and sat down.

"Well, that certainly went differently than I had expected! Why didn't you come in sooner?"

"Um, I thought that you might want to see how the *other* half lives."

"Well, my God! I had no idea that a woman could make me feel such passion! My wife really *is* a frigid hag, you know! I really owe you a debt of thanks, Harry!"

"That's OK Doc. All's I want from you is help with my situation."

"I really hate for you to lose this amazing talent of yours, there's so much you can do with it!"

"I know, I know, but it's an awesome responsibility, Doc! It ain't all fun and games, you know?"

"I suppose not."

The Doctor lapsed into silence as he contemplated all that *he* would do if he could read people's minds. Every now and then he'd look over at Harry, who'd be shaking his head sternly, giving the Doc a chastising look for some thought or another. Yes, he finally concluded, this was an awful responsibility.

"So, Harry, how should we proceed? There's the surgical route or, perhaps, some form of drug therapy would be in order. Although, to stop the voices all together, I think we'll have to treat it like an extreme case of schizophrenia."

"Naw, Doc. I don't want you to stop the voices. I want you to make me stop caring. I just don't want to be moved by the words I hear."

"Well, I don't know if I can do *that*."

"Sure you can, Doc. Just think, you help me, I help *you*!"

Harry listened while the Doc made up his mind. He knew the Doc would help him. He was right.

* * *

BIG BROTHA

It was Halloween. The streets below were filled with screaming hoards of ghouls and goblins; and their parents. From his perch up on top of the hill, Big Frankie watched. He didn't get to town as much as he used to, back in the old days.

"Now that's when they knew how to throw a party!" He mused to himself.

Frankie made himself a sandwich (Black Forest Ham on Rye) and popped the top on another brew, heading back to the "observation tower" for some more fun. His size sixteen Doc Marten's clanking across the floor, littered as it was with a sea of dead soldiers, a veritable carpet of red and white.

"I've got the Blues!" He said to the murky air.

Reaching the "tower", he dialed in the high-powered telescope on the roof and focused it on the town below. The telescope was made by the same contractor that produced the Hubble telescope, back in the early nineties, but, for some reason, this line actually worked. In fact, it worked so well, that the company had been forced to recall the whole line in order to avoid looking like complete idiots with the Hubble screwup! Frankie had gotten someone to pull some strings so he could keep his, but he was one of only a handful to have this privilege.

So tonight, as with all nights, he sat down at the screen and began to "monitor" the town below. It was his town and he felt kind of protective of it. Each night he kept his vigil. Each night he watched for trouble down there on those darkened streets. He "patrolled" the streets around the University, especially the dorms and Sororities, he searched the parks for signs of trouble, and he cruised the Strip for danger. Through the magic of technology, he was able to do this with the telescope because it was powerful enough to see clearly the smallest detail, even at this distance (two or three miles)!

So advanced was this equipment, that Frankie could track areas of potential danger and pay extra attention to them during his evenings. A computer kept track of all the data and it could even suggest areas for examination on any given evening. It really lived up to its name **The Big Brother**, which, as it turns out, is the reason that the Hubble thing happened. It seems that Big Brother was supposed to go to Hubble and the Hubble brain ended up being a monster. That's *Meteor Observation Network System, TeRra;* this was the telescope's original design: to view distant comets from EARTH! Somehow, the two systems got mixed up at the factory, no one knows how (although there is a guy living quite nicely in the South Seas who used to be the Head Engineer on the Hubble Project — everybody else ended up working in the "Games" department at Macroslop, redesigning software).

Anyway, Frankie was settling down to another long night. He went immediately to the Fonda Towers, where the University had set up a temporary dorm after last months Hell Week had led to that unfortunate series of fiery explosions. Because the towers were some twenty-five stories high, Frankie could "patrol" the upper floors easily.

He scanned the windows on the upper deck, pausing, every so often, to watch the co-eds as they moved about inside. Sometimes they were dressed, sometimes not. Sometimes Frankie would watch someone ironing clothes, half dressed, and get more excited than when he would spot one walking around the apartment, nude. Other times, he would spend several minutes watching one of them on the phone, half-naked, talking to God knows who. It sure wasn't him!

This night, as he was scanning the towers, the phone rang!

At first Frankie wasn't sure what that strange sound was (it had been such a long time since he had received a call). Eventually, he realized what it was and answered it. A disembodied voice, sweet with femininity, spoke to him; *by NAME!*

"Frankie? Hi there handsome! How are you tonight? Are you enjoying the view?"

Frankie felt a cold shiver run down his spine. How did she know? No one in the town knew that he was up there, at least that's what he thought. He looked at the receiver as if it could tell him anything. It said nothing. He put it up to his ear, cautiously.

"I think you've got the wrong number sister!" Frankie tried to sound matter-of-fact.

"I don't think so! You're the guy in the sky with The Big Brother, right? Look over at the Towers, the one closest to you, eighteenth floor. Look for a sign and remember, I've got your number!"

The line went dead.

Frankie put the phone down as if it might explode. His fingers drummed the desk top nervously for a moment before he reached for the Joy Stick and moved the telescope to the eighteenth floor of the tower closest to him.

The first window was dark. The next one revealed a co-ed studying. She was stretched out on her bed in her underwear; red panties (Frankie always liked red panties). He panned to the next window where he saw a guy sitting at a computer. Hm, could this be the caller? Naw! That voice was way too sweet! So he kept going from window to window, looking for a sign of some sort. And then he saw it. It was pretty obvious. One window had been completely obscured by white, block letters that said,

I'VE GOT YOUR
NUMBER!

Frankie switched to the next higher magnification. Through the hole in the letter "O" he could see some activity. A girl was pacing back and forth. She was dressed in sweats. She appeared upset. Then Frankie remembered that feature on his phone, the one that lets you call the person back without knowing their number. He picked up the receiver and hit star 69 and waited as it rang, watching the girl, who stood watching the phone ring in the room on the eighteenth floor of the tower closest to him.

"Hello? Who is it?" She said as she picked it up.

"So, how did you get my number?" Frankie asked as he watched her turn suddenly and face the window. He could only see the right side of her torso, the rest was obscured by the lettering.

"Can you see me?" She asked, turning sideways.

"Just barely, those letters are pretty subtle;" he said sarcastically.

"Well, a girl's got to have some privacy!"

"What? You never heard of curtains?"

"Don't bullshit with me! I know that you can still see something, even with curtains!" She hissed.

"Too true;" Frankie mused. "So what's the point of this little charade?" Frankie was getting tired of this interaction. It was making him nervous. It was not supposed to be like this. He wasn't supposed to have any contact with the town. Someone had really screwed up! Heads would roll!

Frankie liked that last part. Heads hadn't rolled in a long time and he kinda missed the old days, when heads would roll at his pleasure. But, those days were gone...

"I want to meet you and you know, date."

"You want to what? Oh, no, that's completely out of the question, no way, no how, un uh!"

Frankie watched her on the monitor. He couldn't help feeling a certain degree of excitement as the conversation progressed, even though he knew there was no way that she could ever get her wish. Maybe he'd even like to "date", though he knew it was impossible. He'd made a deal with the town fathers way back. They'd leave him alone, and he'd stop dropping by for visits. No more carrying off livestock or townsfolk. It had been a hard fought deal, wrought out over

Claudio Parentela

several years. And when the loneliness of his perch had become unbearable, and he had beseeched the town council for some respite, this was the compromise that they had arrived at. And it was fine, had been for years. Until now. Until this.

"What do you mean?" She purred into the phone. "Don't you find me attractive?"

This seemed like a very odd question.

"Other boys find me attractive. Don't you boys find me attractive?"

Frankie looked in the monitor. There appeared to be someone else in the room. He panned over to the hole in the "O" in 'your' and could just make out something moving around on the bed. Frankie moved the magnification up another notch and saw that there were two boys sitting on the bed looking over towards where she was standing. He heard muffled voices in the background and saw one of the boys hold up his hand, making the OK symbol with it towards the window.

Then he saw her hand the phone to one of them. He spoke.

"Hey man, howzit goin'? Listen Carla wanted me to tell you just how hot she is for you! And, believe you me, she is FINE! Really! I don't know about her trip with you, but you have got to meet her because she's got a thing about you. I mean it!" Then he handed the phone back to her.

Frankie was beginning to enjoy this. It was a new twist on his isolation. It was like a game. But all games must end.

"So you see sugar, I'm not kidding. I WANT YOU!"

The boys on the bed were laughing. Frankie began to feel abused. Who were these kids to toy with him? He wasn't their personal mouse, to be batted this way and that. They were just fucking with him. What had he ever done to them? Nothing. They were just bored. He settled down a bit.

"Listen, you little cunt! Don't you and your friends have anything better to do than fuck around with my head?" He growled into the phone.

"Oh, but that's what I want to do! Don't you see? I want to fuck with you, but all I've got are these two boys!" She whined into the phone while the boys howled with laughter in the background.

Frankie began to feel that old fury rising in him. It had been decades since the last person had messed with him. And what a mess he'd made of that fool. They were *still* finding pieces of him! But the unbelievable gall of this little bitch and her friends was almost too much. He wished that he could just reach out and squash them like the slime that they were. The world would be better off without these morons.

"I'd like to fulfill your wish, babe, but I'm miles away from you, as the crow flies, and I'm stuck here. Besides, once you saw my ugly mug you'd know why I'm locked away up here." He was in total control.

"Then I guess I'll just have to come to you!"

"NO WAY! You're just some little girl with way too much time on her hands and not enough excitement in her pathetic little life. I'm not your toy. You don't even mean the things that you say."

"Oh. I don't do I? How can I prove how much I'd rather be with you than with these two?" Again they were laughing at him at his expense.

"Kill them."

It had come out without his even knowing. It had come out down and dirty. Frankie wasn't even sure if he'd meant it. It was just a reaction. This was why he'd been forced to stay out of town. He couldn't control his temper. If something hurt him, he hurt it back, tenfold. If someone fucked with him, why then he'd fuck them back so hard their relatives would feel it. If you threw a rock in his pool, he'd throw one back, but it would be a ten ton boulder!

Then he heard her say, "He wants me to kill you two."

In the monitor, they doubled over with laughter and then stood up giving him the finger. As if this wasn't enough of an insult, one of them moved to the window, slid it open and dropped his pants and turned, shaking his white ass out the window. Frankie could hear them over the phone. This was no longer any fun at all. He hung up. He stared morosely at the screen.

Through the open window he could see the boy shaking his penis at someone, presumably the girl. It wiggled like a piece of hose. It was limp. This was mildly interesting because he hadn't seen anything sexual in a long time, just nudity. He was still, strangely, drawn to this scene, even though they were probably still joking with him. He knew that they'd get theirs from some ball-busting wife with a good lawyer. So he watched. And as he watched he noticed that he felt nothing, as the scene unfolded, he felt neither good nor bad. He merely watched. And then he just zoned out. Zonksville.

The phone rang. Frankie picked it up, startled.

"I hope you enjoyed our little show," she rasped, her voice distinctly animal sounding.

"Oh, I'm sorry, were you putting on a show for me? I missed it. I must have dozed off." Frankie tried to sound indifferent.

"Well, that's too bad, 'cause you missed some hot action! But, don't doze off now. It's the grand finale!" Again he heard laughter in the background.

He looked in the monitor and this time both boys had their little, fluffy asses poking out the windows. As he watched, he could hear them shouting encouragement to her. And then one of them came on the line, so to speak.

"OH GOD! You don't know what you're missing here! Man she can really suck! She's like a Hoover! Oh yeah, baby, do it, DO IT!"

And then it happened. It was unthinkable, impossible, some kind of awful mistake. As Frankie watched the screen, one of the boys toppled backwards out the window! He could hear the screams coming from the room. Frankie moved the joy-stick and deftly followed the boy as he plummeted down the side of the building. It was horribly delicious! About half way down he got caught up in some grill work, briefly, but broke free again after leaving bits of himself behind. Frankie lost him in some other buildings around the fifth floor and scanned back up to the window, just in time to see Carla banging on the other boy's hands with her computer monitor, as he clung to the window ledge, trying not to fall. Finally, she threw it at him with all her might and both he and the monitor went crashing down to the ground.

Frankie was appalled! But he was also, strangely fascinated by this woman (she could never again be seen as a girl in his eyes). He focused on her face, upped the magnification another notch and watched her pick up the phone again. She shook her hair and took a deep breath as if she was composing herself and said, "Well, do you believe me now?"

"Yes," said Frankie, "yes, I believe that you need serious help, now!"

"And?"

"Come on up, Carla."

Frankie waited. In the darkness below he could see the lights of a single car moving up the road towards his keep. It must be Carla. He didn't know what he was going to do when she got there.

Then, as he watched, the lights were joined by more lights. More cars were following her car. These cars had flashing red and yellow lights. This was not good. This meant she was bringing trouble to him. Once again someone was bringing trouble to his door. Frankie continued to watch.

Soon the lights were joined by lights from the sky. These lights shown on the car and the road surrounding it as it sped along. Frankie hoped that she would be able to make it to his door, if only so he could meet her. But he knew trouble would be right behind her, and he had never had a good relationship with trouble. It was just one of those things.

* * *

MAGIC FINGERS

Dusty was sitting at the bar, beer in hand, watching the patterns made by the setting sun as the light shot across the dance floor and bounced off the chrome legs of the railing that ran around the runway. It was too early for the "floorshow". It was too early for much of anything; and it was too late for Dusty. He salted another pickled egg and bit into it. It tasted like Kim Chee, but it smelled like the alley behind this place – stale urine and used palm oil. You know, that rancid smell that all alleys behind restaurants smell like. He fought the gag reflex and choked it down. The beer helped to take the edge off the taste, but just barely. So he ordered a shot.

"It must be five o'clock *somewhere*" he muttered to no one in particular. One must keep up appearances, even in this God forsaken place.

This particular God forsaken place was just another mill town that Dusty now called "home". Soon the rest of the locals would come staggering in, take their usual places at the bar and wait for the girls to come grinding out onto the stage. And he would sit there with a hard-on, watching while they (the girls) dry humped the pole, waved various parts of their anatomy in the upturned faces of the locals and seduced dead presidents from the back pockets of these hard, working stiffs.

But it was quiet now. Dusty liked it this way; sitting in the late afternoon sun, enjoying the peace and solitude. It was almost reverent! Like being in one of those big cathedrals; the air so still and cool. You almost felt like you had to take little breaths. He worked on his beer in the silence.

"Wa guh shub..."

Dusty looked up and to his left. Five stools down, an oriental-looking guy was having trouble staying on his perch. He was plowed. He clung to the bar like it was going to rush away from him, leaving him stranded to balance alone. He had a bewildered look on his face, a look that Dusty had seen before. It was somewhere between fear and abandonment. Dusty had seen it on the face of a dog that had been stranded on a roof top during the great flood of '93. The dog was eventually rescued by some National Guardsmen. Dusty wasn't sure if this guy would be so lucky.

He slid down to see if he could help.

"Say pal, what's going on?"

The guy looked up at him from the bar top, where he had rested his head on his folded left arm. His right arm extended straight out and gripped the gutter on the bartender's side. He was certainly Asian, possibly Thai or Korean. It was hard to tell since his features were blurred, like a face glimpsed through wet glass. He squinted at Dusty as if he was afraid to open his eyes, as if he might bleed to death. It was obvious that he'd been on a bender for some time. Dusty moved in closer.

"Say pal, are you okay?"

"Uh, yeah, sure. Thanks. You plenty crazy stay here, man. You plenty crazy!"

"Me? Crazy? What do ya mean?" Dusty was eyeing the guy with suspicion. His English was pretty good. Must be a college boy or something. Yet he feigned that broken-English crap like he was a coolee talkin' to the bossman. Dusty felt like he'd just drifted into a badly translated Kung-Fu movie. But the Bartender wasn't Bruce Lee, and they were still on American soil, as far as he knew.

"Lissen, man. You wan' know what drove me to this," he gestured grandly with his right hand, letting go of the bar top, briefly, then grabbing the edge of the gutter again with his left, nearly falling off the stool; "it's my gift to women!"

He slapped his hand against his brow, massaging his face in one, swirling motion. This move ended at his neck, which he grabbed and squeezed a couple of times.

Dusty, pausing to consider the implications, thought; "this guy's either a loon or he's psycho, either way I'd better get out of here!"

Dusty looked at his watch, as though he'd just remembered an appointment.

"Geeze! Look at the time! Shit I gotta get goin'. It's been real interestin', pal, but I gotta see a man about a dog!"

He started to move away, but the little guy grabbed his arm.

"Lissen! You probably won't believe me, but I gotta tell someone! I gotta pass on the legacy, gotta transmit my knowledge to someone before I go!"

He pulled Dusty and his arm close into him, and continued in a conspiratory tone.

"I can make any woman happy!"

Now Dusty knew this guy was bonkers.

"Yeah? Well that's great. I wish you luck on your quest!"

Dusty was searching the room. The guy had his arm in a death grip and Dusty needed to distract him, so he could escape. Unfortunately, even the bartender had left for the moment.

"Lissen, pal, you gotta help me, here! I gotta pass this knowledge on before I croak!"

Dusty's hand was startin' to go numb. Oh, well, what could it hurt to sit here and listen to this guy? He probably had some little oriental trick that hadn't made it into the Kama Sutra, which Dusty could use to dazzle his next "romantic" encounter. Besides, the girls would be comin' in soon and the place would start rockin' and Dusty could lose this moron in the crowd. The guy was sittin' in Big Frankie's spot and BF wouldn't think twice about ejectin' his sorry ass out the back door, in a three-wall bank shot!

"Okay, pal! Unloose the arm, you're damaging the merchandise!"

"Oh, sorry."

"Say pal, what's your name, anyway?"

"Huh? Oh, name's Tran, I'm from South Campochia. Been in this country since war, since '78. Went to UCLA where I was pre-med, but got side-tracked by Holistic Health Movement. Hooked up with guy I met in Chinatown herb shop one day. Old fuck, from old country. Old ways, old shit, you know? Genuine article! This guy show me, then teach me ancient art of Acupressure."

"You mean Acupuncture?" Dusty interrupted.

"No, no, Acupressure. No needles! Use fingers in place of needles. He teach me to cure many diseases with this technique! I become student. Forsake UCLA, but still live on campus until scholarship run out. I practice on fellow students. Become very popular with spiritualists, good for ego, not so good for libido. No pussy for non-doctor Tran. Pre-med Tran score many times. Quit program, lose tickee. 'No tickee, no laundry' to quote Hop Sing.

"Anyway, one day am complaining to 'Teacher' about loss of status in 'realm of senses' and he tell me about technique for satisfying any woman. He say technique so powerful, women become love-slave or join nunnery or go insane. Most go insane."

"That explains the rise in crazoids on the streets around here! And I thought it was part of the Reagan Legacy!" Dusty mused to himself.

Tran continued.

"I say to him, 'you must think I'm really stupid! I'm pre-med, for Christ's sake! You can't make any woman happy with just a finger! It takes whole lotta ingredients: Technique, nice car, good money, fashion sense, telepathy, right sized wand; many things!'

"But he say, 'no, you are wrong. You misunderstand what I mean. I'm not speaking about mere physical satisfaction, this is no mere bump and tickle session. I speak of bliss, of becoming one with the continuum, of tapping into the cosmic hey-now!'

"Well, I knew that I was way outta my league, here, so I just shut the fuck up and let him ramble on. He told me tales that would make your skin crawl! He hooked me with visions of unending vistas of cosmic understanding through the realm of the sensual. And the key that unlocked that door was this technique of the psycho-sexual. He regaled me with moral tales, with visions of bliss-filled meditations.

"Finally, I succumbed. I had to have this power over women! I had to learn how to convert every female that I secretly lusted after into my personal love-slave! I had no idea what was waiting for me, once I'd crossed that bridge. No idea at all."

Tran slumped against the bar. He was asleep!

"Great! Here I am, on the verge of discovering this guy's secret and he passes out on me!"

Just then the bartender returned.

"Hey! Help me get my friend outta here, your watered down booze has knocked him out!" Dusty yelled to him.

Together they scooped up Tran and carried him out to Dusty's car. It was getting dark and Dusty had no idea what to do with him. Tran refused to revive long enough for Dusty to get any cohesive info out of him as regards an address, so Dusty started for home.

Some time later, Tran stirred.

"Whaa, what, where am I?"

"Relax, you're in my car and we're almost to my house. I'll make you some coffee and if you can sober up enough to tell me, I'll drive you home. If not, you can sleep it off on the sofa."

They drove in silence the rest of the way.

Back at the shack, Dusty put the kettle on and sat down at the dinette, opposite Tran.

"So tell me, what's involved with this technique?"

Tran squinted at him across the table. He looked awful. Dusty guessed that he wasn't long for this world, or any other, for that matter.

"Oh the technique is easy! I could teach it to you in just a few minutes! But the problem isn't the technique; no, it's in the use of it. It's the judgment that is so important! There are grave consequences at stake here! If you misuse this power, it will eventually eat you alive! It will drive you around the bend! It will drive you to drink! In short, it will take you on a journey from which you can **never, ever** return!"

Dusty thought of that little oriental kid in one of the <u>Indiana Jones</u> movies as he listened to this speech. If this guy could do what he said he could, who cared what the consequences were! Dusty sure didn't. Blah, blah, blah, Tran droned on explaining this and that. Dusty dreamed of an army of love slaves doing his every wish. He remembered a joke he'd heard the other night.

What's the difference between a blimp and 365 blowjobs? One's a Goodyear and one's a great year!

Dusty smiled. And then he heard Tran.

"I see you smile. You don't believe me, do you. You think I plenty crazy! Okay, I prove to you and then maybe you believe this is serious."

Dusty wondered how this was going to work. It was just him and Tran, and he sure as hell wasn't going to let Tran do "It" to him.

"We need subject. I will summon." Tran said matter-of-factly.

"How?!"

Tran stared straight ahead. Clearly, he was in a trance. It was, suddenly, real quiet in that kitchen. Time seemed to be slowing down, stretching out, like taffy being pulled. Dusty felt himself falling or, maybe it was, floating. He liked this sensation. He'd never have to buy any intoxicants again! *Coolness!*

The knocking door brought him back. Dusty had no idea who it could be, especially at this late hour. He opened it up. Standing on his porch was a woman who lived down the street. She was not someone he had ever really paid much attention to before. What did she want?

"I wanted to borrow a cup of instant coffee," she said.

"Let her in," Tran said from behind Dusty's back.

Dusty stepped back from the door. The woman entered, stiffly. She navigated the room like she was under a spell. Dusty thought of the zombies in The Night of The Living Dead, a campy and badly acted movie from the fifties. A love zombie? *Double Coolness!*

She sat down next to Tran. He gestured for Dusty to stay over by the sink. Then he stood behind the woman, placing one hand on her shoulder with the fingers spread loosely, and the other hand hovered over her head. After a few moments, Dusty noticed that Tran's breathing had become very calm and regular, not rough and raspy like at the bar. And then Dusty noticed that her breathing was beginning to match Tran's.

There was something very appealing to this breathing technique. Dusty felt an, almost, reverential feeling come over him as he watched the woman's chest rise and fall through the fabric of her blouse. He, too, began to breathe in this manner.

"First step: breath must be same, in sync." Tran spoke clearly, almost serenely.

Dusty could not move from his spot, nor could he take his eyes off of the couple, but he sensed that the room was beginning to change. As if the paint was changing color and all the hard edges were becoming soft ones. Dusty remembered the taffy again. And he was floating again, in fact, they all were! *Triple Coolness!*

"Next the trance is achieved."

This is great! Dusty thought to himself.

The room began to pulse, that is to say, the light in the room began to pulse. Dusty noticed that the lights was decreasing and increasing along with his breathing. He also noticed a throbbing in his ears, almost like a generator coming to life somewhere far away. Then a strange thing happened. A wave of sensations swept over Dusty: first he felt like he was running very fast; he felt exhilarated and physically, he felt a jolt of adrenaline burning through him. Next, he felt as if he was lost at sea, bobbing on the surface like a cork. Up, up, up he rose and down, down, down he dropped; the fear was intense but there was also a glimmering hope, of all things. It was crazy and perplexing and wonderful! Then, he felt this tremendous sense of well-being and security as if the ocean had turned into a pair of strong, yet gentle, hands holding him, protecting him, keeping him safe from any harm. All the while, the lights pulsed on, seemingly driven by their breathing. Tran and the woman were still at the table, but to Dusty, they appeared two dimensional, like an old photograph.

Then, he heard the door. He blinked. Somehow he was standing at the door, turning the knob again. He opened it. There was an older woman who looked vaguely familiar standing with an empty cup out there.

"I've come to borrow a cup of instant coffee." She said.

"Let her in." Tran said to him.

This is a weird deja vu. Dusty thought.

The woman walked into the kitchen as if she'd been here before and Dusty followed. Tran gestured for her to stop.

"Hello." He said to her.

"Hi." She answered.

"Do you know me?" He asked.

"Should I?"

"Do you know him?" He pointed towards Dusty.

"Only in passing. What's your name, again?" She asked Dusty.

"It's Dusty."

"Oh, yeah. Say, Dusty, could I borrow some sugar?"

"I thought you said you wanted some instant coffee?"

"Perhaps, she'd like a cup of coffee, a cup of instant coffee?" Tran said, emphasizing the word instant. Dusty automatically moved to the stove to get the kettle. He hadn't like the way Tran had said instant but he wasn't sure why, either.

"Why, thank you!" The woman said as she slipped into the chair next to Tran.

Dusty poured the hot water into a cup and added a spoonful of coffee to it. He turned and took it to the table. The woman reached over and lifted the cup to her lips, sipping cautiously. She put the cup down quickly and tried to conceal the expression on her face. There was a word that described this face. It was UGH!

"If you wouldn't mind, could I have some sugar?" Her voice was sultry, almost liquid, with just a hint of a Swedish or, was that Texas, accent. Dusty knew her from somewhere, but he couldn't quite place her; Mrs. Something or other.

Tran jumped up and reached for the cupboard where Dusty kept the sugar, just as Dusty was reaching for it.

"Let me get it for you!" Tran exclaimed.

This Tran guy was pretty spry for being on his last legs.

Tran leaned close to Dusty and said, "Go, ahead and touch her. Do it anywhere it won't matter. You touch her now."

Tran gave him the sugar bowl. Dusty looked into his eyes. There was something there, something that bordered on hopeful yearning, with just a hint of terror. He made a mental note and turned to face the woman. She sat expectantly. Dusty could almost picture a thought balloon forming over her head. It said:

"Yes?"

"How's that coffee?" He asked, thinking he would sound forced, but surprised at how easily the words came out.

"Oh. It's the richest kind!" She exclaimed, almost jolly.

Dusty set the sugar bowl down. He felt very odd, as he watched her put

53

two spoonfuls of sugar into the cup and begin to stir. He knew he knew her from *someplace* but where? There was a feeling of expectancy mixed with malevolence in the air, as if she was an innocent fawn about to be crushed and destroyed. He felt guilty, almost satanic, as if he was the slobbering beast who would make this happen, an ogre full of smutty ideas and intentions, all fang and claw, ready to pounce out from behind this facade and take her six ways from Sunday! Yet, she continued to gaze up at him pleasantly enough.

At least until he put his hand on her shoulder. Then her look slowly dissolved into one of fear, followed by exhilaration, and, finally settling on a cool desire. This melted into lust rather quickly. The next thing, Dusty knew, she was leaping into his arms, her mouth tossing out words, as if to clear some room for something else.

"Oh, God, I want you, now!" She rasped in a husky voice as thick and furry as a tongue after a three day drinking jag.

Mrs. Olsen! He thought as he wrapped his arms around her ample frame.

Then, she was on him. Her hands moving over him like a tree full of squirrels on speed. His tongue shot into her open mouth like a stiletto into tapioca pudding. They fell to the floor, grappling like a pair of shoppers at a lingerie sale. Tran watched them grunting and rolling around on the floor for a while and smiled. Then he left. Mission accomplished.

* * *

HAND JIVE

"Hello?"

"Yes, who is this, please?"

"Mom, it's Billy."

"Billy? Is there something wrong? You sound so very odd? You're not in trouble again are you?"

"No mom, I'm okay, in fact I'm more than okay, I'm great, really!"

"Then what is it? Why are you calling?"

"I'm calling to tell you some great news, mom. I'm calling to tell you that, after years of searching, I have finally found my soul-mate..."

"Who?"

"MY soul-mate! The woman of my dreams! I'm engaged, mom! I want you to meet her; I want to bring her over to the house this weekend so's you and dad can meet my fiancé!"

Billy's mother took a deep breath. This was more information than she was used to dealing with, especially from her errant son. For years, she and Mr. D. had hoped and prayed that Billy would settle down and get a real life. For years they had watched in horror as he went mindlessly from one stupid relationship to the next; watched while he drifted into every fad, every stupid little gimmick that came down the pike.

Billy had tried it all in his search for his "SOUL-MATE"; he'd tried every kind of therapy that could be imagined and quite a few that didn't seem to have anything to do with the realm of love at all. He'd tried Past-lives therapy, Primal therapy, Pet therapy, Post Traumatic Distress Syndrome Therapy (even though he'd never gone to Vietnam or any other war);and he'd tried Gestalt, Jungian, Analysis, Empathetic, Rolfing, Reichian, Colon and Semi-colon therapy; and he'd tried all sorts of drug therapies, though most of these were not administered by a professional. And then there were the sexual "therapies"...Billy had had the nerve to ask his own mother and father to finance his therapy with a "doctor" who was nothing more than a Pimp in an office with nice art in the waiting room and some fancy looking diplomas that hung on the wall over his desk which was next to a bedroom set, complete with headboard and end tables.

Apparently, the "Doctor" would have Billy act out his sexual fantasies with one of his "nurses" while he observed, took notes, and sometimes even videotaped the sessions! When they had found out about this little escapade, Mr. D was so upset he had to join one of those Public Warehouse Wholesale Clubs just so they could start buying Mylanta by the case!

"Just a minute, Billy, let me switch to the other phone...."

"Okay, mom."

Mrs. D. poured herself a shooter of Mylanta and tossed it back. As she walked back to the phone, she thought about Billy growing up; it was a stream of bitter-sweet memories. She wanted to believe him this time but she knew from experience that she'd have to be wary, she'd have to be unimpressed and distant and it tore her up to be like that, because, unlike Mr. D (who could turn it on and off at will), Billy's mother really wanted her son to find what he needed so much....a soul-mate. And now the tears were

welling up in her eyes , DAMN!

"Are you okay ?"

"Yes, Billy, I'm okay."

"Are you sure, Mom, you sound like you're crying."

"Oh Billy, I'm just so happy for you, that's all. Your father and I want to meet your fiancé as soon as possible, say, Sunday? Let's make it for lunch, okay?"

"Lunch is no good, mom. What about mid-afternoon?"

"Okay, that's fine, we'll see you then. Goodbye son."

"Goodbye mom."

As she hung up the phone, Mrs. D. could feel the tears begin to fall. She regretted not using the waterproof mascara, but then, one couldn't always be psychic.

"Mr. D.! Mix me a double Bloody Thursday! In fact, make yourself one and let's get plowed! Billy's coming for cocktails on Sunday and we better start getting ready for his next hair-brained idea."

Billy hung up the phone and turned to his fiancé; "Well, we're on for Sunday afternoon at my parents'."

"That's great! Is there anything more I should know about your parents, honey?"

"Well, yeah. My parents and I went thru a lot of bad times when I was younger and they're still kinda suspicious of my grasp on reality. But don't worry, I know when they meet you, they're gonna see that I was right and that you are the soul-mate I've been searching for all these years."

As Billy had been saying this, his fiancé had laid her head on his lap and was gently mauling the beast that was stirring inside the cave made by his opened zipper.

"Oh, Billy! Give me your Willy!"

Billy sighed and happily complied, thinking as she descended; "All this and she's a poet, too!"

Upon hearing his wife's news Mr. D. had started drinking so heavily that he had been forced to call in sick for the rest of the week (it being the day before Bloody Thursday-ironically). By Friday, both of the D's were so wiped out that one of their friends, a shrink that they had met during the course of one of Billy's "treatments", had come over to stay with them and administer "B-12" injections on an hourly basis just to bring them both around for the meeting! The good Doctor had even gone to the local P.W.W.C. for a case of Mylanta, some Tomato Juice, a 1/2 gallon of Vodka, a couple of bottles of Viseene and a case of tissues. He also picked up a ten pound bag of Porterhouse steaks, a couple of bottles of Red Wine, some Tums and a cashier (who was having problems with her boyfriend and needed some advice) for himself--a kind of professional gratuity for his troubles.

So, after a brief consultation in a Cheap Six Motel room where he brilliantly and concisely laid out both the cashier's problem as well as the cashier herself, and after stashing the steaks, etc. at his pad, he headed back to the D's for further "therapy". Mrs. D looked like she could use a good consultation, herself.

By Sunday morning, after using a bottle of Viseene per eyeball, eating Aspirin like it was candy, and some very disturbing dreams about a doctor, an enema bag and a pickle, Mrs. D. was attempting to tidy up the house while Mr. D. sought solace in the morning news on T.V.

By lunch time, they ate their first meal in almost two days. It was a light meal, their tummies being somewhat jumpy from their respective jags. Mrs. D. was very hungry, but her lips were sore and she couldn't seem to put anything in her mouth without becoming flushed.

"Great!" She thought; "Menopause..."

"How do I look, Billy?"

"You look great"; Billy said as he tucked in his new La Crosse Polo shirt.

"Careful, you'll wrinkle my dress, honey!"

"Oops! I guess I'm kinda nervous."

"Well, you just let me do the talking and I'm sure that your parents will like me once they get to know me."

"Yeah, you're probably right."

Billy rang the doorbell. He could detect the muffled sounds of activity behind the door. He reached for the doorbell again. His finger hovered over the gilded plastic rosette, as if the button would open the yawning, greasy mouth of Satan and they would all be sucked down his gullet as easily as one sucks oysters off the half-shell.

Just then the door opened and framed in the doorway, with their lovely Ethan Allen, Early American style furniture as a backdrop, stood Mr. and Mrs. D. looking very much like the couple in that painting "American Gothic" with the emphasis on the THICK part.

"Come in! And where's that cute little gal that you've been raving about?"

Billy's dad had suddenly developed a dangerous Tex-Arcana drawl.

Billy moved thru the screen door as if he was leading someone, someone so petite that his one hundred and eighty pound frame twisted sideways could conceal them.

"Oh my God," thought Billy's mother," he's fallen in love with a midget!"

"Mom, Dad," Billy started the speech that he had spent hours rehearsing:" I know that I have been a great disappointment to both of you over the years. I know that you've always hoped that I would grow up and make something of myself, and that you never believed me when I said that I would find my soul-mate and then I would be complete. Well, I've finally found her and I want you to get to know her as I do. I'm certain that once you've had a chance to talk to her, you'll see why I'm so happy. She's everything I've always dreamed of. So let's sit down on the sofa and I'll let her do all the talking."

Mr. D. rolled his eyes at Mrs. D. as if to say; "Here we go again!"

They both turned and headed for the sofa, where they sat down and looked up at Billy who was standing next to the matching loveseat, still with his arm behind his back.

"Mom, Dad, I'd like you to meet my Fiancé."

Billy's arm came out from behind his back and time slowed way down.

Mrs. D., her mouth moving like a freshly landed and very exhausted Bass, leapt from her chair and headed for the kitchen. It seemed to take hours. She grabbed the bottle and clawed desperately at the top, but was unable to free it's calming contents. She panicked. But over her shoulder, she heard the reassuring, though unintelligible, tones of her husbands voice:

"I've got it honey!"

Mr. D. grabbed the bottle from her hand and masterfully broke the top of the bottle off, just below the cap, with the flat edge of the Ginzsu Butcher's Knife that had just arrived in the mail that week. He poured his wife a generous double shot, as well as himself, being careful not to get any glass in the Mylanta. Then, looking his wife straight in the eye, he toasted her, tossed down the anti-acid and said; "I'm gonna kill that lousy bastard and dance on his grave!"

But Mrs. D. intervened, as always, the calming voice of reason.

"Mr. D.! Let's at least hear him out and then we can have him declared legally insane and get him out our hair forever !"

Mrs. D. had positioned herself between the doorway and Mr. D. with her arms outstretched like she was trying to flag down a car. Mr. D. was still flexing his grip on the Ginzsu, waiting for her to be distracted so he could use that move that had won the Big Game back in '49.

"Besides you won't have to go to jail for murdering your own child!;" Mrs. D. pleaded.

This was sobering. Mr. D. thought about the counseling sessions and the hours of commiserating he'd have to do with guys named Bubba and Leroy, not to mention the humiliation of the trial with all the scrutinizing of his very limited personal life.

"Okay. I'll hear him out, but I still want to hurt him!"

"Of course, dear; we'll both have to 'subdue' him before the authorities get here!"

They were both lost in the reverie of this idea for a brief moment and then they headed for Billy.

Billy sat on the loveseat with his "fiancé". His parents sat across from him on the sofa. It was very silent for a long time.

"Mom, if you'd just let her explain....."

"Shut up, son!"

Both Mr. D. and Mrs. D. were giving Billy's girlfriend the Mother of all Hairy-eyeballs. They were profoundly moved by the level of depravity that their son had achieved this time. For what Billy had produced as his fiancé, was a hand-puppet! Well, a glove really; a white glove with a blond wig sewn across the top of the knuckles, with a pair of eyes, one on either side of the first knuckle and some very large, red lips attached to the side of the thumb and the index finger. But that wasn't the end of it. No! Hanging down below the palm of the glove was a little body, like a rag doll's, only slightly more shapely! They had seen this before, thirty years ago on the Ed Sullivan Show.

And now as they stared in disbelief, Billy began to stroke the hair of this thing, and as he did so his hand actually turned and stared up at him, as if it was actually enjoying the attention!

"ARE YOU OUT OF YOUR MIND?!

Billy's dad had cleverly set the stage for the pending insanity plea he would use at the trial.

"Why no, Mr. D., Billy's not crazy at all, in fact this is the best possible solution to the problems of being single in the nineties!"

Billy smiled at his parents; he knew that his fiancé would be able to present them with a very persuasive argument, and it looked like she was going to win them over.

Billy's parents were flabbergasted. They had no idea that Billy knew anything about ventriloquism, for as they stared at him, the HAND HAD BEGUN TO SPEAK!

And Billy's lips never moved. This was great! He really was insane and from the looks of it, it was a complete and total job! They'd have no trouble booking him a space on the "Rubber Truck" for the trip to the state run booby hatch. They looked at each other happily, as though a great weight were finally being lifted from their shoulders. But their reverie was short lived, as it was broken by the HAND.

"You should really be happy for your son, because he's finally coming to grips with this crazy world that we, you and I – the hand is actually referring to itself as a separate entity – live in. I know that you both are alarmed by the increasing level of irrational behavior all around us. Mr. D., you're always complaining about how concerned about the criminal presence in the neighborhood you are! And you, Mrs. D., aren't you always saying that you don't understand this modern world, what with all it's so-called time-saving devices that don't really save any time at all?"

The D's looked at each other, all three of them. The hand made sense. But it was just a hand, for Christ's Sake! Lucid or not, it was still attached to the very demented wrist of their demented son! But the HAND was unrelenting. Billy moved his arm up and rested it on the back of the loveseat at eye level so that the body of the HAND draped down, it's little legs resting on a Persian-style pillow that Mrs. D. had picked up at the Akron twenty years ago (when Billy still was showing some promise). Mrs. D. began to wonder if this was how Moses had felt when confronted by the Burning Bush and the ensuing conversation that followed?

"Billy has told me about all the trials and tribulations that he, as well as you , have been thru and I think that you should thank your lucky stars that he hasn't turned out really weird!"

" Now just a doggone minute, you..." Mr. D. started in;" what do you, you...." He looked at Billy, exasperated. "Billy, what the hell do you call your 'fiancé'?"

"Rosie;" said Billy without even blinking.

"What right have you got coming in here and subjecting us to this charade?!"

"What right have I got? I want to make Billy happy and I can. And I'm not just talking sexually, either. Mrs. D. you know, as well as I do, that men can be kept in line with a little 'action', but there's a lot more to it than that. Men are like children, they need supervision. For example, I picked out Billy's new shirt. Nice isn't it?"

"You know, Rosy has a point, Mr.D;" Mrs. D. found herself saying; and she wasn't agreeing just to get on Rosie's good side (like she found herself doing so often in the past with Billy's other girlfriends); no, she knew that there was truth in what was being said. Besides, she *did* think that the new shirt looked very good on her son; a definite improvement over the old "T" shirts that he normally put on.

"Is anyone thirsty, besides me?" said Mr. D. as he headed into the kitchen for more Mylanta.

"How about mixing up some Bloody Mary's for us, Dad?" cried Billy after him.

The afternoon went by very quickly, as the D's opened up more and more to this new stranger in their lives. Billy let Rosy do most of the talking, chiming in occasionally with a comment or two. Mrs. D. and Rosy chatted it up quite nicely and were becoming fast friends, when Rosy revealed that she planned to marry Billy in June (three months away). This stopped the conversation, but nothing like the revelation that it would be a full, formal wedding in CHURCH and with a reception to follow. Time stopped.

Outside the house, birds were frozen in mid-flight, passersby in mid-step, planes hovered in the air. In short, for a brief few seconds all movement on the space-time continuum ceased. And in that awful, agonizing moment, the

D's realized *again* that their son was crazy, crazier than a loon. Had the "M" word not been mentioned, or, had a small, private and discreet service been planned, the D's could have handled Billy's eccentricity. But, NO! No, he had to go wreck yet another chance at reconciliation with his mother and father!

It was nearly midnight. The D. household looked as if a tornado had just gone thru it. Mr. D. sat on the edge of the sofa, the telephone cradled against his head, as if he was having a conversation, but the line had long since gone dead. He had the look of weariness that one might see in a Walker Evans photograph – one of those Great Depression shots. He called it the "old man river" feeling – 'tired of living but scared of dying'. His hair was messed up and his shirttail was out on one side, as if he had been in a brawl, which wasn't too far from the truth.

Mrs. D. was in the kitchen, head buried in her folded arms on the kitchen table, still sobbing, one hand clenching a highball glass filled almost to the brim with Vodka. A patina of tomato juice floated on the surface. It was her third and final drink.

Elsewhere in the city, Billy was staring intently at a fluorescent light trying to go blind. The hospital room that the good Doctor had booked him into was very private, very clean, very white and very safe. Restrained at the wrists and ankles, strapped down at the chest and mid-section, Billy was hardly in a position to do much more than stare. He had been heavily sedated when he first arrived, protesting that they couldn't separate him from his true love, his;" SOUL-MATE!"

The good Doctor had proved him wrong. With the easy practiced hand of a surgeon; a man who had performed countless lobotomies, a man who had deftly removed thousands of pairs of surgical gloves, not to mention pantyhose and other undergarments; he had divested Billy's lover with one quick gesture. Billy sank into another world, where he and Rosy frolicked amongst wildflowers, with butterflies and tweeting birdies.

"See, Billy, it's only a glove, a ball of material, a piece of fabric, a dust rag, nothing more."

But as the Doctor was saying this he couldn't help noticing that the hand puppet was cleverly made, and he begin to think; "Hm, this could make a very interesting case study! I could write an article for the Journal Of Deviant Sexual Behavior and present it at the AMA convention in Las Vegas next year! Hm,hm, hm!"

Taking the puppet back to his office, his mind ran ahead with his pending rise to medical stardom: he could open a series of clinics nationwide to help the sexually dysfunctional, he'd be on the cover of Time, People, even Psychology Today! He'd do the Talk Shows, he'd do Phil and Oprah and Maury, he'd even do (dare he even think it possible) Regis! Oh yes, this was going to be his meal ticket out of this dump of a hospital! He'd have to get to work on *this* right away.

As soon as he got to his office, he started to compose the article. He called in his assistant, an overly developed Candy Striper volunteer with whom he had been "consulting" for about two months and asked her to take notes. She sat on the edge of the psychiatric couch, notepad at the ready, her hand poised. She had been thru this drill before. She knew that he would start to dictate and she would start to take notes, and that he would describe a "case" involving some form of sexual fantasy or deviancy and that soon the details of that "case" would become so lurid that it would be very difficult to concentrate on her task and she would ask for some water which would always mysteriously end up getting spilled on her dress or on his pants and so on. So she was not surprised when he began to dictate this time, although he didn't even wait for her to sit down before starting.

"God!" She thought; "He must really want it bad tonight!"

The Doctor paced back and forth for over an hour, but the details never got very juicy. And although she did detect a certain swelling under his lab coat, he seemed to be more interested in the rag he was carrying, than in the fact that she had managed to hike her skirt up to her hips without using her hands.

Finally he stopped pacing, looked down at her legs, paused and said;

"You look tired, why don't we take this up in the morning?"

She was stunned. She stood up and headed for the door, adjusting her skirt as she went.

"But Doctor, aren't we going to, um, you know....."

He had been sitting on the couch as she was leaving and as he leaned backwards, she noticed his obvious erection. He held up his hand as if he might be asking her to stop, as if this might be a new twist on the old routine, but all he said was;

"Goodnight, see you tomorrow."

Well!

The Doctor held up the rag admiringly and said;

"You are going to make me a rich man!"

And then he thought; "I'm talking to a piece of cloth as if it was alive...hm, this is very interesting. I wonder what Billy ever saw in this thing, anyway. I wonder what his mindset was when he put it on."

"Why don't you try me out, Doc, and see..."

The Doctor looked around, self-consciously. He was alone; except for the puppet. But he could swear that someone had spoken. He went back to his musings about the workings of the delusional mind. Without even thinking about it, he casually slipped on the glove and began a light-hearted make-believe conversation with it.

At first, he talked to the glove using the old Gestalt technique of projecting a fantasy personality onto an inanimate object; but soon the glove was telling him things about Billy that he could never have known, things that Billy only knew in the dark recesses of his sub conscience. The Doctor began to get anxious. He was losing control of the situation. So he turned to the one thing that always worked in situations like this, he turned to sex. While the glove regaled him with tales of Billy's hopes and dreams, he unzipped his fly and pulled out his penis. He waved the thing at the glove, tauntingly and said;

"Meet the meat!"

The glove seemed to want to move towards his penis, but he was actually straining the muscles in his arm to restrain it; and he was losing the battle. It wasn't like arm wrestling with yourself, the glove was alive. The Damn thing was ALIVE! And so was his penis....

"Oh my God!" Two voices exclaimed simultaneously!

The glove/Rosie was devouring the root of the Doctor's power and he was powerless to do anything about it except lay back and surrender.

As he neared, what he knew would be the best orgasm he'd had in years, he heard the glove whisper in his ear;

"Let my Billy go free and I'll fix you up with my sister; she makes me look like an old maid!"

"OH GEEZUS YES! DON'T STOP! I'LL DO ANYTHING YOU WANT, JUST DON'T STOP!!!"

Out in the hall, at the nurses station, that last line had been heard by the night nurse and the custodian. They both exchanged knowing looks.

"I hopes the Doc don't hurt hisself;" said one.

"You gotta admire a man who's willing to work so hard to help some-one find true happiness!"

"I jus hopes that I don' hav'ta clean up some kinda mess....."

Sometime later, around 3 or 4 AM, after the Big Bang had subsided and the molecular structure of the Doctor and his office had reconfigured into their original forms, the Good Doctor slowly climbed back to reality. Somehow, he had ended up, half on the floor with his legs drooped over the "couch" which, in turn, had somehow ended up on its side. His clothes, or what was left of them, were still damp from sweating and there was a distinct line running straight up from an oval shaped pool in the middle of his chest. He tipped his head backwards on the rug and saw the mark on the side of his desk where a million tiny travelers had died immediately following the Big Bang. There were also several spots on the carpet, and, judging by the boney taste in his mouth, apparently on his face, all deposited by the arcing head of his trouser snake as it spit it's venom across the room.

He was still panting slightly, as if he'd been on the hunt and had just returned.

"So, you mentioned a sister?"

The glove stirred in the dim light.

"Does this sister have a name?"

"Her name is Heather and she's into leather!"

If it was possible to have goose-bumps on one's penis, then the Doctor knew he had them.

"But first you must free my Billy. When he and I are safely away from here then I will send my sister, Heather, to you. Not before!"

"But how do I know that I can trust you ?"

"Well Doc, how do I know I can trust you? By the way, Doc, you got a cigarette?"

The Good Doctor rested his head on the carpet and wondered how he could get the upper hand (as it were) on this situation. The idea of delusional transference was a passé cul-de-sac in popular psychology, but *this* involved delusional animation on a primal subconscious level. He had studied many deviant behaviors in his time, but he had never seen, or heard of, anything like this before. He had to study this phenomenon more closely. He had to milk the situation, somehow.

"Heather can milk you until your balls implode!"

"My God! You can read minds, as well?" The Doctor felt very vulnerable all of a sudden (as if laying on an over-turned couch with his pants around his ankles and cum stains from his chest to his desk wasn't enough).

"Some are easier than others; yours is a very quick study."

The GLOVE was very droll.

So, for the next several hours, the GLOVE and the Doctor plotted Billy's miracle recovery.

It was agreed that a gradual recovery would be best to avoid suspicion and to allow the Doctor a chance to study this phenomenon more closely. The Doctor had to promise to return the GLOVE to Billy for at least a few hours each day, for 'nurturance'. Also, the GLOVE wanted someone else in the room whenever the Doctor was "curing" Billy. The Candy Striper was the logical choice since she already knew of the Doctor's eccentricities and would not be too surprised by the procedures involved.

Further, the Doctor had to promise never to reveal the identity of Billy so that he could live his life out with dignity and privacy. Any papers, books, video or audio tapes, any format that his research took would have to omit the identities of all involved or there would be some very dire consequences. The GLOVE detailed what these consequences might entail and was so convincing that the Doctor was inclined to kneel before the porcelain God for a good fifteen minutes.

At 4:35 AM he fell asleep. He dreamed he was the "Flying Dutchman", a mighty square rigged ship, plowing through the waves, the GLOVE at the helm, steering him through stormy seas the rest of the night, using his penis like a tiller.

Six hours later, when the Candy Striper arrived at the Doctor's office, she found him at his desk working on some notes, quietly humming to himself. She had never seen him in such a sunny mood before (mornings weren't very good for him usually). And the office was much brighter, and, except for the spot on the rug where something had been spilled (funny, hadn't noticed that before!), cleaner.

And the Doctor was different. He sort of glowed! And as far as she knew, there was only one reason for such a look! So, with a jealous flush in her cheeks and her nostrils flaring, she stalked into the room.

"Just what the hell's been going on!?"

The Doctor looked up from his desk, jolted out of the dreamy state of recollection. Advancing towards his desk was one pissed-off, yet highly charged and very erotic, young volunteer. He had never really appreciated her (probably because he had never really seen her) before. He realized that he had used her body as a vessel for his carnal needs without ever appreciating her own attributes. He couldn't even remember what her body looked like or how it felt to enter her or if she gave good head or what her lips felt like or how she tasted or anything!

He was at once, amazingly turned-on by her presence and ashamed by his own greed. He was also astounded by the fact that he was actually experiencing a moral dilemma! He'd read about this but had never really understood what it meant.

"So! You promised me you'd never screw anyone else in this room!" She hissed thru clenched teeth.

"What a contemptible, lying sack of shit I've become!" The Doctor thought to himself; noting with further amazement the apparent birth of a conscience.

She had reached the edge of the desk and was rounding it, when she suddenly grabbed the letter opener and said;" Why I oughta Bob-bit and feed it to you like sushi!"

To her own amazement, the Doctor pushed his chair back, unzipped his fly and with tears in his eyes looked up at her and begged her to relieve him of this terrible burden.

"Please help me and just hack the damn thing off!"

And with that, he pulled his battered cock out. They both looked at it. It looked like it had gone two rounds with Mike Tyson. No, it looked like it had been hit by lightning. Wait, it looked like it had been run over and dragged down the street for a few blocks. In short, it looked dead.

"Aw, you poor little thing, what's happened to you?" She said as she picked it up and cradled it in her hands. As she leaned over, the Doctor got a whiff of her perfume and a wave of excitement washed over him, the first of many sets to come.

The penis played dead. The Doctor watched as his assistant examined it. The assistant picked it up and looked it as if she was appraising it for auction. She tickled it and petted it, she stroked it and pinched it. She looked at the Doctor and said;" It's either broken or dead, either way it's not gonna do anyone any harm anymore!"

"Maybe it's like Sleeping Beauty?" He offered.

"More like Sleeping Ugly!" She countered. Then she leaned over and kissed it. The second wave caused it to stir.

By the fourth wave the thing was attempting to stand; and by the sixth wave it was up, wobbling back and forth, like a newborn calf. And she knew it was hers, at last.

She stepped back, unzipped her uniform and let it drop. She unhooked her bra and let it drop. The half-slip fell away and she stepped naked from the heap of clothing. She never wore panties, at the Doctor's request. Now she advanced on the Doctor and straddling him, grabbed his cock and pressed the tip against the moist entrance of her pussy. She waited and watched the Doctor's face. Little hints of emotion played across his cheeks and eyes like the shadows of clouds blown across a windy landscape.

She waited. She was waiting for his submission, waiting for him to run up the white flag. And slowly, she began to see signs that her siege was working. As her grip tightened, and her own excitement became apparent, she noticed beads of sweat forming on his brow and temples; and a certain flaring of the nostrils. She noticed the breath quickening and his lips parting just slightly. His eyes began to plead with hers, but no sound came from his mouth. She leaned close to his face and looked into his eyes, deeply, and waited.

The Doctor found himself in quite a fix. He wanted her bad but he knew that she wanted him to say he wanted her and this would mean... well, what would it mean, exactly? He couldn't think clearly, he wanted her badly but he didn't want to surrender his pride; no, his power. Yeah that was it. And there was something else, something in the distance, just barely glimpsed.....something he had forgotten. It was Heather. He knew that no matter what she did to him, the GLOVE would take care of him. One way or another.

"So fuck me."

That was all she needed to hear. She descended on him like the Mongol Horde descended onto Europe. And much like the Horde, she sacked and looted and raped and pillaged him. But unlike the Horde, she didn't leave him in ruins when she was done.

Somewhere between her fourth and his third orgasm, Billy popped into the Doctor's minds eye.

Billy lay in bed, strapped down, with EKG and EEG wires attached to his chest and forehead. In his mind, he floated on a thin, white cloud, far above the turmoil of the world below. Billy was so heavily sedated that he didn't even know what the Doctor was waving in front of him.

As this was the first session in Billy's "Recovery", the Doctor wanted to go very slowly. He had carefully explained to Candy, his assistant, what the plan was: namely to re-socialize Billy so that he could function in the "real" world without having to rely on the delusional girlfriend manifested in the form of a GLOVE/puppet; or some such crap (at least it sounded good)! He had explained to her about the GLOVE, but she had been repulsed at first, followed by disbelieving and then curious. He knew that he couldn't demonstrate on himself, although the idea of a three-way with her and the GLOVE did excite him greatly. But he also knew that she still had that letter opener!

So now he gently waved the puppet in front of Billy's face. No response.

With Candy scribbling notes, as she monitored his vitals, the Doctor gently slid the GLOVE onto Billy's hand. No response. He carefully removed the wrist strap and stepped back. Nothing happened. He looked at his assistant, then he looked at Billy and then he looked at the GLOVE. Nothing. He didn't understand. Then it happened.

One of the monitors beeped. The GLOVE stretched like a cat and began to move towards the middle of Billy's body. Billy was still out of it, yet his hand moved on. as if it had a mind of it's own; as if it was mortally wounded, dragging itself to some safe haven; the wounded Lassie returning to its master. And as it crept, it dragged the hospital gown up. The Doctor reached down and pulled the gown up over Billy's waist. Candy scribbled faster. She was trying very hard not to lose her objectivity, but it was very hard to stay focused. It wasn't as if she'd never seen a patients genitals before, these things happened every so often. During her four years at this particular hospital she'd seen all kinds, some gargantuan, some bent, some bowed; mostly, though, they all looked like sausage in the flaccid state AND it was damned hard to get it up when you were on MEDS--it was damned hard to do anything on MEDS!

But Billy's exposed penis, though still soft, seemed to be stretching towards the hand puppet, as though some invisible force was pulling on it! And now, here came the GLOVE. The meeting of the two was like a soldier returning from the war to his wife. They embraced and they embraced and the GLOVE began to massage Billy's "sausage" which was rapidly becoming a Polska Kilvassa!

Wiping the little trail of drool that had begun to seep from the corner of her open mouth, Candy quickly turned to study the monitors, which were going crazy. Even though Billy was still out, on the surface, there were all kinds of activity going on. Both of the monitors were registering vital signs that indicated a tremendous upheaval was underway; possibly as a result of the tension created between Billy's sedated brain centers and this surging sexual energy. She'd never seen anything like it before. She was getting worried. His heart rate was spiking irregularly and his breathing was shallow and rapid. She turned to the Doctor.

"Doctor, I don't think he can handle this!"

"No, but I think you can!" And with that, he snatched the notebook from her hand and pulled her over to the edge of the bed.

"We are going to try a little experiment. I'll pull his hand away and as I do, I want you to take over."

She looked at him like he was crazy. He wasn't crazy, just crazed. He was flushed and there was a frantic look in his eye, which she had seen earlier. Still, she knew that this would help stabilize Billy and she didn't want him to get hurt. So, she reached down and, mimicking the hand, began to masturbate him. At first, this worked fine, but as soon as the GLOVE was no longer touching Billy's skin at all, his penis went flaccid. But, as soon as they placed the GLOVE back near his penis, why it swelled right back up in her hand. Droop-swell, droop-swell, on and on for several minutes. Finally, she let go.

The Doctor peeled the GLOVE off Billy's hand and left for his office.

Candy looked at Billy while she adjusted his gown. He looked so angelic. She brushed his hair out of his face and gently kissed him on the forehead. She paused at the door to look back at him briefly, and then she closed the door and went down the hall to the Doctor's Office.

When she got to the Doctor's office, she found that he'd started the party without her. She sat down and watched him. She thought that he was a jerk for preferring a puppet over her, but as she watched, she found herself getting hotter and hotter. Eventually, she found her way over to him, and, squatting down on his chest, let his tongue go exploring. It looked like he was going to get his threeway after all.

Over the next few months, the Doctor was able to wean Billy from his obsession with Rosie the Glove. Mostly he had employed his own variation on Aversion Therapy, a technique that turns the patient's favorite thing into something that makes the patient violently ill at the mere thought of it. In this case, the Doctor enlisted his assistant as the 'wedge' between Billy and his puppet. Fortunately, though it seemed unfortunate for the Doctor at the time, Candy was able to forge a bond with Billy and soon this bond grew into love, as deep and profound as any epic love story that had ever been told.

Even Billy's parents had come to love Candy as if she were their own daughter. So, it was a very happy day, indeed, when Billy and Candy announced that they would wed in the fall. Everyone was elated by this. Mrs. D was amazed at Billy's miraculous recovery and Mr. D was amazed that the Good Doctor hadn't charged them an arm and a leg for his remarkable work on their son. Even the Doctor was amazed at his unexpected altruism (though he secretly knew he would get his reward soon enough from the wicked Heather).

So, one night, as the Doctor was preparing his paper on Billy's deviancy and subsequent cure, he took the glove out of his desk drawer and put it on. He was seeking its wisdom, consulting with it, as it were, as he had done many times before when he found himself 'blocked'…Usually it was a quick tussle and once he'd cleared his head, he could get back to work. But tonight it was different. The glove seemed despondent (if such a thing was possible).

"What's the matter?"

"I miss Billy;" the glove responded.

"Well, you knew it was part of the cure we worked out. It was your idea, as I recall."

"I know, but I really miss him."

"Well, you'll be back with him soon, after he marries Candy."

"That was supposed to be our wedding;" the glove trembled as if little tears would fall from its little "eyes".

The Doctor found himself moved by this plaintive statement, but could he risk reintroducing Rosie back into Billy's world without there being dire consequences to his recovery? There had to be a solution.

"I need to see you in my office, Candy."

When Candy entered the office she was surprised to see the Doctor sitting at his desk, wearing the glove. Over the past few months, she'd seen him wearing the glove, but it was usually after the event, when clothing was in disarray. Now, the Doctor appeared to be talking to the glove in a low, conspiratorial voice.

"Ah, there you are. Come over here and sit down, we have something to discuss with you."

We? Candy didn't like the ramifications of that. But she sat down next to the desk, anyway.

"Candy, I've discovered a potential 'fly in the ointment'. But I've come up with a plan that I hope will be both amenable and effective. As you remember, the reason you and Billy met in the first place was because of this;" at which point the Doctor pointed towards the glove.

"Yes, Doctor, I do."

"Well, there's been a snag in the therapy and the glove and I want to bring you on board, so to speak."

Candy looked at the doctor skeptically but kept listening. As he laid out his strategy, she couldn't help but think that he was really crazy, himself. But as he went along, she knew it would work, as crazy as it sounded. And she knew she had to go through with it because she truly loved Billy and wanted, more than anything else, him to be happy.

In the end, she agreed with the plan. If nothing else, it'd make a good story...

On the day of the wedding, as Billy nervously stood at the alter with his best man (the Good Doctor, who else?) waiting for his bride to come down the aisle, he wondered about this strange and crazy road that he had traveled down to get here. Who could have imagined how this would have turned out? Certainly not Billy. He looked over at his parents sitting in the front row, beaming proudly at their son, so proud of him for turning his life around in such a short period of time.

Suddenly a surge of adrenalin shot through him. What if this was just a drug induced dream that he was having? He felt a little woozy and started to tremble, but the Doctor grabbed his arm and said, "It's all right Billy, just a little while longer, be strong."

Well, if it was a dream, it was pretty good. Just then, the organist started playing the Wedding March and Billy looked up to see Candy moving down the aisle towards him. She looked like an angel. Seeing her like that made him stand up taller, he was so proud. The doctor loosed his arm, knowing that Billy was going to pull this off. He thought of Heather and noticed that he was standing taller too.

The ceremony was simple and poignant. The bride and groom exchanged vows that they had written and even the most cynical present (the Doctor notwithstanding) found they were moved by the sincerity of the words. Billy recited a poem he'd written when he first realized he'd fallen in love with Candy, who smiled (a bit forcefully, perhaps) through it all.

After the "I do's" and the kiss, the happy couple marched down the aisle and out the door to the limousine, which whisked them away to the home of Mr. and Mrs. D for the reception.

"Whew! I'm so glad that's over with;" Billy sighed as they got into the limo.

"Yes. Now all we have to do is survive the rest of our lives together;" said Candy.

They both looked a little sad for a moment. Then Billy got a little teary eyed.

"What's wrong, Billy?"

"I don't want to tell you;" he sniffed.

"Come on, you have to...remember what the Doctor said?"

Billy remembered that the Doctor had made him promise that he would always tell Candy his secrets or else he'd have to go back to the hospital.

"All right, but I don't think you are going to like it very much...I was just thinking about how, before I met you, I had planned to marry...Rosie! This was supposed to be OUR day. Now I guess I'll never see her again, even if seeing her makes my tummy feel icky."

"Oh, Billy. That's so sweet!"

"It is? I don't understand."

Candy was reaching into her purse, searching for something. Billy thought it was her hankie, but it looked more like a...

"Rosie!"

Candy cautiously placed the glove in Billy's hand, making sure he wasn't going to get sick. The last three weeks before Billy was released from the hospital, the doctor had been, through hypnosis, conditioning Billy to accept the gloves presence without getting ill. There was no way to guarantee that it would work or that Billy wouldn't revert back to his "relationship" that he'd had before he met Candy. But Candy had come up with an idea of her own that she believed would compensate for any power that the glove might have over Billy.

Billy trembled as he looked at the glove. Oddly, he didn't feel nauseous at all. He noticed it was now wearing a tiny version of Candy's wedding dress.

"Go ahead, put it on. I have another surprise for you."

As he worked to put on the glove he noticed that Candy was doing something with her back turned towards him. Then she turned her head and with a sly smile, said, "Ready?"

She turned to face him and extended her left hand towards him. She was wearing a similar glove like his, only her's had a tiny tuxedo and a little top hat. Billy raised his gloved hand and touched hers. In an instant, they were locked in a mad embrace. Billy kissed Candy, Rosie kissed her new boyfriend. At last, it all made sense.

*   *   *

Hey Elmo Get a Loada This!
Or how I Forgot the Horrors of 9-11

When the façade was vaporized off our little Norman Rockwell world, that is to say, when nine eleven happened, I was visiting friends in Washington State some thirteen hundred miles from home. I remember being glued to their TV set watching hour after hour of raw video being beamed into living rooms all over America on that first day. It was hypnotizing and horrible all at the same time, much the way a traffic accident draws so many rubber-neckers – you feel compelled to look, even if you don't want to see anything. The whole country gawked at New York City, in all of its murky devastation. And I gawked right along, from the second tower sporting an unseasonable orange chrysanthemum to the blizzard of ash and confetti to the search for the wounded to the search for survivors to the eerie sense that things would never be the same again.

Every time I closed my eyes for the next six months, a parade of images from those initial fifteen hours, cascaded through my mind's eye. It was frightful. I knew that there were others who felt the same way, because I'd had conversation with them. And then, one day in March 2002, something happened to change all that.

I received an invitation to have dinner with a friend at her mother's house one Sunday evening and out of guilt I accepted. See, I was trying to get 'chummy' with my friend and she had indicated that this would happen a lot faster if I went with her and pretended I was her beau (a sort of stunt-boyfriend). My friend, Priscilla, didn't see her mom very often because, as she told me, frankly, she was kind of hard to take in large doses (ironic, because her mother wasn't very big, but when it came to outlandish behavior, she was a giant!). But I'm jumping ahead of the story.

My own mother was slowly dying of cancer at a famous doctor's hospital (where she was receiving excellent care – at least until her insurance ran out), and I was down visiting her from my central California home.

My friend's mom, Karen, lives in a coastal town west of Los Angeles, in the same house that Pris (as I call her) grew up in. She got it as a prize for putting up with her husband's philandering ways, if you know what I mean. She lives there with her boyfriend Floyd. Pris tells me they have been living together for over twenty years! For some reason her mom will never set foot in a church again, at least not for her own wedding. Like Tom Waits says, "I don't mind weddings, as long as they're not my own!"

They make quite a pair, Karen and Floyd. They've been living together so long that they operate like a tag team. Floyd'll start a sentence and Karen will finish it. She tells a story and Floyd does 'color commentary.' Floyd tells a joke and she tells the punch line. It's a very down-home, yet eclectic atmosphere.

As we sat in the dining room just off the kitchen, I looked around. Her mom had a fondness for contact paper (you used to be able to buy it at Target or the Akron...it came in all these bright colors or looked like "authentic" wood grain – we used to call it hillbilly wallpaper) and she used it extensively. Oddly though, she also made a mean flower arrangement and apparently picked up some folding money doing arrangements for some of her friends and events down at the Bingo Center. Yeah, she's a regular at the center a few towns over, and the way Pris tells it she's practically the belle of the ball. Truth be told her mom talks like Longshoreman...but the gals at Bingo would never know, 'cause Karen leads a double life.

Oh yeah, did I mention that she drinks? She's been putting the booze away for quite some time...and Floyd ain't no slouch in that department either. In fact, every year for at least the last fifteen or so, Floyd and some of his friends have made their own wine. They drive a couple of pickups up to the wine country and bring back a couple of tons of the grape and mash 'em, bottle 'em and put them up in her mom's garage to ferment. It's quite an operation. Just picture that episode of I Love Lucy where she decides to go native on a trip to Italy and ends up brawling in the wine vat with one of the local gals. The only difference here is that if there's any brawlin', it's over who gets first taste.

So, on the occasion of our little party, the vino was ready for sampling and we commenced to sampling. I have to say also, that homebrewed wine packs a wallop since it is usually at least five percent higher in alcohol than the store bought stuff. So two glasses is like drinking three or four, depending on your tolerance. Pris told me later that you need a lot of tolerance to sit through a dinner at her mom's house, hence you need a couple of glasses of wine, or gin, or whatever it is that allows you to sit numbly by while Floyd tells his racist jokes and Karen tells her stories about how screwed up the country is.

Well, by the time dinner was started, we were a pretty happy crew, feeling no pain as the saying goes. Pris is usually pretty jovial. She has a contagious laugh which causes her to jiggle a bit when she gets going; and, by this I mean that like most women who reach a certain age, they tend to end up on the round side, what I'd call *zaftig*. We all tend to get a little thicker around the middle and I'm no exception.

I was filling Pris in on my mom's condition, which was pretty serious, when Floyd headed out to see if he could put the meat on the grill. In this case it was steak, a nice thick cut too, served with salad and potatoes and, you guessed it, another glass of wine. Karen just sat there like a bump on a log while Pris and I calmly discussed the impending departure of my mother. It'd been a drawn out process and we were both (Mom and I) looking forward to its end. At some point in the conversation Karen started relating a story about one of her friends who was suffering the same fate and as she droned on I found myself drifting off into my own little world of thoughts. I couldn't close my eyes and rest because when I did that, there was that damned tower with its orange "flower" suddenly blooming...

Fortunately, Floyd brought the steaks in from the BBQ and dinner began. The conversation moved away from death and dying and became more irreverent. As Pris had warned me, her mom began her litany of people who'd disappointed her, with her kids being at the top of the list. I wanted to protest and get on Pris' good side, but said nothing because I knew from my own mother that it was pointless. I'd been down this path before and knew that my sibs weren't worth the effort required to defend, either. Besides the steak was great and the wine was providing a cotton candy-like layer of tolerance, so I just let 'er rip. And rip she did. She ripped Pris (who just smiled politely), she ripped Floyd (who chuckled and said "it's true"), and she even ripped me for "settling" for someone like her daughter (I thought I saw just a glint of anger in Pris' eyes but she kept on smiling). She went on and on like a little kid having a tantrum and we sat there like hostages, wondering when the axe would come down.

Eventually, Karen ran out of steam and slumped into her chair. I asked Priscilla how her day went (me artfully pretending to be her boyfriend) and she gladly took charge of the conversation, but again I found myself drifting off. She's very active and does a lot of traveling for her job, so she's always coming home late. I know this bothers her, but she takes it all in stride (which is probably how she handles her mom's outbursts) and smiles through it all. She's a sly one, old Priscilla. God, I love her.

Somewhere during this chatter, maybe after dessert and coffee, we got to talking about this fellow who has a show on the local PBS TV channel, called Travels With Elmo. He sounds a lot like a cross between Gomer Pyle (a character from an old TV show who had a big smile, a back-woods drawl that just wouldn't quit and a fondness for saying "Shazzam!" when he was impressed by something) and Floyd. He's got this persona that just seems arcane in our "modern" world. It's "golly this" and "golly that" and "gee whiz" etc. Elmo travels around the state and does little puff pieces on towns and people that are off the beaten path. His show is interesting sometimes, but he's so over-the-top that you almost need a big, old, glass of "tolerance" to watch him.

There we sat, relating our favorite episodes, mine being the one where Elmo and his intrepid cameraman Luigi ("Golly, Luigi, look at that!") go to a borax mine and see these huge dump trucks and I did my best impression of Elmo drawling "Golly Luigi, look at the size of those tires!" Floyd chimed in, "They's huge!" And we all started cackling with laughter. This went on for a while until Karen got that devilish look in her eye. She nodded her head towards the door-way behind me and said to no one in particular, "You know what I'd do if Elmo

Claudio Parentela

was standing over there?" She leaned back in her chair, puffed out her chest and, to my horror, started bobbling her boobs up and down, saying excitedly, "Hey Elmo, get a loada this!"

You know how time slows down when you're in peril, like during a car acci-dent? That's what this was like. Try to imagine the sight of an old lady cackling her ass off and bobbling her tits, which are really just sacks of skin so they don't really bounce anymore, but really just go flap, flap, flap. Now add to that the fact that this old lady is the mother of someone you desperately want to get close to and you get some idea of the shock I was in...I wanted to scream, but Pris beat me to it; "GEEZUS H. CHRIST, MOM WHAT ARE YOU THINKING!?!"

So, as she kept flipping those things, I turned to Pris with a look that was pure "Silent Scream" and mouthed the words "you owe me." But old Priscilla just smiled that Cheshire cat smile back at me and arched her eyebrows just slightly as if to say, "hey, this is my family, deal with it!" I knew she was right and it dawned on me that if I played this right, I'd be collecting from Pris for quite some time.

This went on for no more than twenty seconds, but it seemed like a life-time. A moment later, after the hysterical laughter died down, I made my move.

"Geeze, look at the time!" I blurted as I jumped out of my chair; "We've got to get going!"

I kissed Pris' mom on the cheek and waved goodbye to Floyd, and before Pris could protest, had grabbed her by the arm and was heading out the door towards the car. The drive back to Priscilla's house was very quiet, neither of us saying anything, especially about what had just transpired. But as soon as I got inside her front door, Pris showed me how grateful she was that I had been there to take some of the heat.

After a few days, when the shock had finally worn off, I told a few people about this incident and I soon discovered that most found it both disturbing and hilarious. This was interesting to me, so I began to study it. I studied it for about a week and *that's* when I discovered something else. I noticed that *now* every time I closed my eyes, I no longer saw that damned tower coming down. Instead…you guessed it, I saw Karen's things flapping up and down. 9/11 was now just a crappy memory (and like any memory, it comes and goes according to its own timetable).

I still find myself laughing sometimes when I hear her words, "Hey Elmo! Get a loada this!"

*   *   *

THE MANX TALES
(Excerpts from the series of the same title)

MANX TOUCHES THE MAGIC

Manx drove through the city, listening to opera. He wished he had a convertible. On days like this, he would put the top down and cruise through Hollywood, a big, nasty redhead sitting next to him. He could picture it with such clarity. He'd crank up the stereo; she'd tilt her head back, shaking out her hair and they'd both laugh as he drove her back to his palace above the Yamoshira.

But he only had his baby-shit brown, Mazda 626 and his stereo. And his opera tape. So on he drove with Puccini and Verdi blaring out of his speak-ers. Manx liked to listen to opera when he drove through the city. It gave the drive purpose and a sense of drama. It gave the gridlocked traffic a reason to exist. You'd have to go a long ways to find anything that would make traffic palatable, but he had, at least, found something that made it more tolerable.

He hit the downtown interchange just as Madame Butterfly wept for the return of her sailor boy. The chromium and glass towers, shimmered in the late afternoon sunlight like so many disco-balls, their mirrored windows casting rectangular images on neighboring buildings, illuminating the canyons of concrete and asphalt below. Negotiating the inter-change was trickier because the glare of sunlit bounced off every speck of dust on the windshield and blinded him. Manx raised his hand in protest. It didn't help.

He thought about the redhead, again. He was suddenly horny. Then, he flashed on the number of times he had driven through this interchange, alone. It must have been hundreds, even thousands of times: trips into the city on business or to see a friend or score some dope. He began to drift into the memory lane. A montage of fantasy and reality danced across his mind's eye, as his imagination fluttered like a monarch from one moment to the next. The stereo blasted out the other butterfly's delicate song. Even the buildings seemed to sway in the late afternoon breeze that swept eastward towards Duarte and Pasadena.

Manx was suddenly immersed in melancholia as the Mazda scooted through traffic. He couldn't help feeling the rising pathos of the aria as it headed for the crescendo. He allowed himself to be buoyed upwards, the hairs on the back of his neck, the goosebumps on his skin and his heart rate: all rising, as if in rebellion.

He rolled down the window and inhaled the air slowly. He held it and then let it out. Manx let the magic touch him, once more.

PLAYING WITH FIRE

Manx leaned over. It felt as though he was leaning out over a great chasm; as though he might slip and if he did, would cascade into the debris below, a long drop into pain. And death, if he was lucky, 'cause no one would want to survive such a fall and have to live out their days as a lump of unrecognizable flesh and hair; a freak-show exhibit.

He leaned out still further. He knew that it was dangerous but still, he wanted to taste the nectar that he knew was waiting in the crevice just out of his reach. He could almost taste it, now, and the idea of its taste, its smell, its feel (oozing down his beard), all this was driving him mad with desire.

He searched the stony face of this cliff for some clue, something he could grab a hold of to keep from falling, from tumbling into the valley below. His fingers were soon woven into a tuft of weeds, perhaps Buckwheat or Desert Sage, like firmly attached straw flowers (like a nappy mane). Manx moved closer. He was nearly there, nearly upon the glistening nectar, he could almost smell the sweetness of the charged air.

He hung there, with his toes rooted in one world and his fingers grasping with the strength of ten, in another, stretched between like a clothesline with a single sock, his desire dangling in the breeze. It felt so good until he realized how vulnerable he was, until the terror began to creep over him like long shadows on an Autumn afternoon. A sudden vision of himself lying broken and discarded on the valley floor, jolted him from his reverie.

He shook it off.. He knew that he could just reach in and scoop out a handful of nectar, were it not for the BEES! He knew that he could succeed but he was afraid that the bees would descend on him in a stinging cloud of vengeance, and that the rocks below would crush whatever life was left out of him.

So, he would have to move cautiously. He would have to become a spider, moving inch by inch, across this crag until he reached his goal, until he could slip his desire into that sweet nectar and taste the ambrosia that waited there for him, alone.

Manx leaned over. He was open. He was ready to receive. He was prostrate in the house of worship, ready to taste the sacrament, ready to burn his lips on the rim of the grail. He was on fire. He would burn for as long as it took, as long as it was necessary. He smoldered as he waited. He had all the time in the world.

MONSTER

Manx read the letter. The words stung like a load of rock salt; like an ulcer flaring up. The words were harsh, cruel and vindictive.

Unfortunately, a part of what was written had the ring of truth. At least, part of him wanted to believe it was true...that he really *was* the monster that was portrayed in the missive. In that part of his brain, he envied the monster, because even a monster was something to be feared, to be pitied, to be caught and studied. And, most importantly, a monster was alive! A monster had passion and strength (and because of this a monster was unpredictable).

In that part of Manx's brain, the monster even had an identity: "Little Man" AKA "You little monster." Little Man was a remnant from Manx's youth, when all adults seemed like monsters, big, scary monsters who doled out trouble on a whim. In Little Man's world, he was *always* surrounded by monsters.

Manx wished the Little Man would just grow up! It's true, that once he had lived in a world of monsters, but then he grew up and the monsters got smaller (as he got taller) or they ceased to be monsters at all. But Little Man just wouldn't let it go. It was like being attached to a ball and chain, only the chain was continually "morphing" into different kinds of nightmarish burdens. One moment it'd be a Kenmore washer on permanent "spin cycle" with a lone tennis shoe inside; then it would become a snapping crocodile; then it would be a pallet of quivering bodies, fresh from the slaughterhouse,; then a field of daisies; then a house with a picket fence and a couple of brats in the front yard, a dog, a 30 year mortgage, the "little woman" waiting...always waiting! He had to snap out of it.

The letter in his hand fluttered to the floor, a forgotten idea. He leaned against the window and placed his free hand across the top of the open sash, his chest resting against his arm, his eyes closed. He sighed. The sun warmed his face. He remembered his mother hugging him on a particular day, back when he was still living in the world of monsters; how she would pull him into the warmth of her bosom and squeeze him emphatically and say, "Ah! There's my little monster!"

He wondered how he could get rid of this particular part of his psyche. The rest of the package was pretty well-balanced. Sure, he knew he had his moments, but who didn't?

"Show me a person without some flaws, and I'll show you a statue;" someone in his past muttered, a disembodied voice hidden in his memory, like a heckler's shout from a darkened theater.

He began to drift from thought to thought like a bee drunk on honey; a woman drunk on love or…a monster, drunk on blood! Damn! He couldn't let his guard down for a moment; Little Man was always waiting in the shadows for a shot. He could ride the coat tails of *anything*. And that letter was like getting an invitation to the Grand Ball! It left a whole in Manx big enough to drive a Semi through. Little Man had slipped out before Manx even new he was on the loose again.

"Where is that little monster of mine?"

Again, the motherly voice and this motherly grasp of heated ozone became too much for his daydream and Manx opened his eyes. The sun no longer felt so friendly. Little pins of ultra-violence were stabbing into his unprotected skin. He squinted, shocked by the brightness. Focusing on the view out the window, he watched a group of people across the street, harassing a dog. They had the dog pretty much surrounded. It didn't look good for the dog; but he had a certain degree of style, and it looked like he wouldn't go down without leaving them with a few bad memories.

Manx turned and reached for something. When he returned to the window, the crowd was closing, like a fist, around the poor beast. He could see their angry faces, looking more resolute and self-righteous with each step. He adjusted the scope and exhaled slowly.

The dog lunged forward, looking in Manx's direction just briefly before sinking his teeth into the nearest leg.

The report of the rifle resonated through the crowd like a bad mood. Order collapsed like a really bad metaphor or a special punch-line. Chaos stepped up to bat, taking a couple of practice swings.

"Ah! There's my little monster!" Manx thought as he chambered another round. He inhaled, then exhaled slowly, squeezing the trigger like a mother hugs her son. It was the least he could do.

His aim was true at last.

HOT BOX

Manx leaned into the hot wind, cupping his hands over the match, trying to light what might well be his last cigarette. Between the howling wind and the screaming nightmares, he hadn't slept a wink last night. Now he was here, pale and shaky, sweating off another hangover at the blast furnace door.

He closed his eyes and waited for the ghosts of his past to appear. They approached him tentatively, like deer entering a clearing, cautious, hesitant, wary. They could be spooked so easily and then they would disappear into the darkness again. He took a slow, hard breath.

He glimpsed one, then another. He froze. They were coming right up to him, checking him out, looking for a clue to his identity. Like guests at a thirty-year reunion party, they waited for their eager memories to catch up with the dull aching throb of this being that reminded them of someone they had once known. Manx wanted to play dead, but that would hardly fool *the dead*, now would it?

Somewhere in the back of his mind, perhaps near the reptilian brain stem, in a room off of Terror Street, a woman's voice began to rise and fall in a melodic kind of moaning. It was as if, Mahalia Jackson had taken up residence in his head to brush up on her spirituals. She knew that no one would disturb her up in that lonely room.

He tried to picture the room. It was dimly lit. The grimy light sifted through smudgy panes revealing walls, unremarkable except for the ghost-shadows where pictures had hung, decades ago. The room had a musty, human smell; a delicate perfume of angst, hunger and weariness. He had visited this room many times in the past, staying briefly, a day or two here, a couple of weeks, there. But since Miss Jackson had taken up residence, he'd stayed away (out of respect); there just wasn't enough room up there for both of them.

Lately, he had begun to feel as if he was being backed into a corner by his thoughts; penned in, or crowded out. As if his thoughts had taken form and were rebelling against the repressive regime that he had come to represent. Manx tried to fend them off, but then he was just succumbing to the madness, defending himself against himself. Even he knew that *that* was pretty silly. So he was forced to resist the temptation to respond and learned to breath through his eyes and not move at all, even to blink. Eventually, the ghosts would move on and eventually, so would Manx.

THE DANCE OF THE IDIOT FLESH

So I was working my way through the stations of the cross this morning and I found myself in front of Our Lady of Macarena and I couldn't remember what to do. Is it right hand to left shoulder, first, or left hand to right shoulder, first?"

"I think it's right over left, first, but I'm not sure."

Manx stood quietly in the shadows of the scaffolding. Somehow he had wound up at the Bradbury Building, that ornate, wrought iron monster near downtown. Above his head the iron intertwined into thick knots of blackened steel, glazed with a thin patina of rust, reddish-brown like the adobe over on Olvera Street. It was as quiet as a tomb.

It was like that part of the woods that grand-ma always warned you not to go into, full of brambles and goblins and other nastiness. He struck a match and was startled by the biting rasp and gush of burning sulfur as it echoed through the hallways. He lit the cigarette and inhaled. He could feel the smoke as it assumed the shape of his lungs. It felt good. Exhaling, he watched the smoke envelope his torso, as if it was trying to get back into his lungs. Unable to penetrate the layers of clothing and skin, it hung around him like a rejected suitor, petulant and sulking.

The two women had passed beneath him on the first floor on their way out the front door. Their conversation was vaguely religious, but, then it was the season for that. He watched them go as he French inhaled the smoke (for that second nostalgic tour of duty). It made him feel cool and mysterious and a bit light-headed. The whole place made him feel kind of edgy. Manx liked this. He needed to hang out in a place like this to keep his paranoid 'chops' up to par. There used to be others, like the Pike down in Long Beach, but urban re-development had picked them off, one by one.

Over the years, this life he lived had gotten bland and he had grown to accept it. He lived in that part of town where the excitement was provided by high-speed chases on their way to another part of the county, to an ignoble, six o'clock, "this just in..," breaking news flash.

Manx wasn't alone in his malaise. The whole town seemed to have grown weary, as if it had just given up and was waiting for the 'wagon' to come. It was inevitable. The city was grooming it's populace to become mindless drones; sweating their lives away, as complacent idiots will do, too ignorant to know that they were making their beds in the devil's mouth. Everywhere that he looked, he saw the signs. Everywhere.

It was especially obvious in the static nature of the shop windows; always so subdued, so difficult to gauge the season's progression...combining that with a climate that was very even-tempered except for a few stormy weeks in the winter. All this made for a very subdued urban environment.

Fortunately, there were always a few citizens ready, willing and able to step out of the shadows and keep things from getting too dull. But they, too, seemed to be unwitting pawns in the greater devilish design. That's why Manx preferred the solitude of these places.

These were the lonely places. They spoke a secret language that Manx could hardly understand. A dark and primal language that drifted through his brain like a pack of miscreants out for a night of mayhem.

The lonely places drew him into them. He returned to them, instinctively, like a swallow returning from Mexico. Only he did it more than once a year. Somehow the isolation stirred a great passion for life in him. It made him keenly aware of it's fleeting nature and it's intrinsic value. The bullshit was stripped away and in it's place was the heady clarity of a pure, clean adrenaline rush. It was consistent and potentially addictive. Like 'crank' or 'crystal' or 'rock'. The state allowed it in small, highly monitored doses in the various forms of sanctioned excitement: the tube, movies, sporting events, Vegas, a good blow job.

But for Manx, these were just fleeting moments on the way to the final embrace. They held little fascination for him, except, maybe, the last item. Apart from that, he found himself a lone sentinel, observing this life, recording it in his mind's eye, for what purpose he knew not. But he did it, anyway. What else was there?

DUALITY

Manx stared at the wall. The pictures of people and places and some things covered it like wallpaper. The pictures looked vaguely familiar but he wasn't sure why. He liked the arrangement of them and there was a certain association that made them flow, as if there was an inherent, evolving theme to their arrangement. In fact, the whole room had a kind of accidental charm to it, as if the random placement of the items had a logical and subtle purpose. He realized that this room was really found art, an accidental architecture whose simplicity innocently disguised its pragmatic functionalism. He stepped to the center and appraised the room.

This *is* nice, he thought.

And it was.

And then he realized why it was so nice. It was nice because it was *his* room, in *his* house, on *his* street, in *his* town. And very slowly, like a winter thaw, it dawned on him that he must be out of *his* fucking mind! Manx stood in the center of the room, a look of stupid wonder spreading across his face like gossip at a beauty parlor. How could this have escaped his attention? Was he really losing his mind or just his identity? Were they the same or were they different? More importantly, would it really make much of a difference in the long run?

He looked at the pictures again. They were places that he'd been to or places he'd like to go to, or places that looked interesting, but that he'd never get around to. The pictures, in fact all the stuff in the room had one primary purpose, and that was to serve as a reminder, a talisman, as it were, of things that existed in his head. Ideas. These were physical links to the many worlds that existed inside his brain.

So, if he had a choice as to what he'd want to lose, which would it be, his identity or his mind?

Without his identity, he'd still be able to create stories about the things around him. In fact, the pictures might be even more interesting if he had no personal connection to them. On the other hand, if he had no connection to this room, he might be inclined to just move it on down the line. Hm. Both sides had merit.

He lit a cigarette. The smoke rose around him like dust from a collapsed metaphor. No, it was clear that neither of those two ideas was an option. The best thing to do was to just snap out of it. Once again Manx had missed the boat philosophically, but had saved his pragmatic ass to fight this insanity one more time.

FALLING ANGEL

M anx sat on the edge of the bed. The empty bag of "Lime 'N Peenyo Chips" (his dinner) lay on the floor at his feet. It was Sunday night. The TV had ceased to be interesting and he now stared at the empty screen, where moments ago lives had flickered and pulsed. He hit the 'on' button, then the 'off' button, power on, power off. The two positions made little difference. He lit a cigarette. In the dark, the glowing tip reminded him of something he had seen recently, something he had glimpsed out of the corner of his mind's eye. He leaned back on the bed and watched the smoke as it curled lazily towards the ceiling.

What was it about the glowing tip that plagued him so? Where had he seen those shapes and colors before? What did they remind him of? Was it the dying embers of a fire? Yes, that was it, and, something else...something like a field of red coals scattered across the black velvet of night. Yes! It was the panorama of Los Angeles at night; the cityscape glimpsed from atop the carpool lane on the one-ten near USC.

Manx had just seen this, not two days ago. The peaceful solitude of the flat-lands of south-central, the lights glimmering as if God had knocked over Lucifer's BBQ, scattering coals everywhere. The city with thousands of points of light. Vegas had Liberace, but L.A. had his cape on a grand and celestial level. L.A. sparkled on this clear night, alive and proud; a vibrant lady, the city of the angels.

He sighed contentedly, took another drag on his smoke and watched it as he exhaled. Soon enough it would be tomorrow and soon enough he'd be facing down another long corridor of work. Fifteen hundred feet of unpainted molding waited quietly in the dark for his patient hand to bring it to life, waited in the dark like a mugger, ready to tick off the minutes of each hour, of each day, marking time until he was dead or the weekend came again.

Either way, Manx was dying, like the embers of that spilled BBQ, like that desire to get up and *"do it all over again, amen"*; the words to The Pretender washing over him, *"Caught between the longing for love and the struggle for the legal tender..."*

He knew it was only a matter of time before his debt would come due; only a matter of time before the day of reckoning would be upon him. Tears welled in his eyes and again the weight of his lonely existence closed on him, again he imagined the cold embrace of the grave. He stubbed out his smoke and faded into sleep, even as the smoke faded into the night.

Desire in A Flat

Standing on the sidewalk, outside the Terminal Bar near the corner of Fifth and Vermouth, Manx pounded another nail into his coffin. It was midnight. Everything shook loose in this town 'round midnight. Inside, Charlie Barnet was blowin' a fat, rich sax on the juke and it was spreading like molasses across the empty dance floor. It was prom night for the hawk.

Outside, that tired old melody lay down on the sidewalk and waited for the clop-clop of death to reign up to the curb and take it away from all this. This delicate moment was lost on the crowd of late-night losers and literary stumblebums, who shuffled past on their way to Palookasville. He wasn't sure where Palookasville was, but he'd heard that it was down by the Harbor, somewhere between Wilmas and the 'Island'. Judging by the burn-outs that he'd seen thus far, it wasn't *anywhere* that he'd like to be.

But then, he was never where he'd like to be. He was always somewhere he'd wished he wasn't. So it goes.

The street was littered with the leftover scum that the cops had failed to rehabilitate in Night Court. A skinny hombre named "Frito" circled around him like a shark with the seven year itch. He sniffed the air for that first sign of fear. Manx avoided eye contact, knowing that he'd have the first dance with Mr. Machismo if he did. Hombre malo. *Muy bad medicine.*

Manx caught a glimpse of his face. He looked like a weasel. Manx had known a guy down in the harbor, once, who looked like a weasel. Was this his son? While he pondered this, the weasel moved off, still hungry. He had an itch that only murder could scratch.

In the distance a dog barked.

Someone leaned on a horn, impatiently, as if they were taking an unscheduled solo. The city pulsed and throbbed to the rhythm of the night with a horn section provided by the intersection of the one-ten, one-oh-one and ten-west. The City of Commerce was taking an extended drum solo and the MTA provided a Bootsy Collins-bass line, as it bored through the guts of the city.

Manx thought about that, about how the city was being gutted by a giant subterranean mole, even as he stood on that street, with the denizens of the dark. Even as the little dramas unfolded behind the walls of the buildings around him, even as someone begged for more and, elsewhere, someone begged for less. Even as Frito was scratching his itch and an act of revenge was being plotted. Even as the moon cycled slowly overhead, making its way back to an early retirement trailer park at Paradise Cove, even as the sun was gassing up for that long pull over the Banning pass.

He thought about God and the atomic clock, about the universe expanding like the air escaping from a blown-up balloon, suddenly released and whooshing recklessly around. *If this was true and the universe was really like a balloon, Manx wondered what would happen when the air ran out?* What would happen to the balloon? Worse still, *what would happen to us?*

He let out a long, low whistle of amazement.

It was midnight and the night was young.

DIRT

Manx stood in the center of the vacant lot, surrounded by dead weeds, crumpled aluminum cans, which shimmered in the midday heat, parched and shiny. An old tire lay near the corner, abandoned after years of loyal service, forgotten like an old man in a rest home. Here and there, tiny shoots of life were sprouting, like the bits of hope emerging after a riot.

A path bisected the lot running on a diagonal, a shortcut that shaved seventy feet off the journey around the corner. About halfway across the lot, very near to where he now stood, two shallow holes, midget graves, were slowly eroding into ruts.

He kicked the ground with his boot. It was hard like the faces of the men who stood in front of the casual labor hall, waiting. They waited, always. They were timeless and empty, waiting for someone to buy their time and put them to good use, like this lot. There were many such lots in L.A. and many such men. Waiting for a resurrection.

He leaned over and scooped up a handful of dirt. It was dry and gritty, like a mermaid's nightmare. It turned to smoke and suddenly blew out of his hand. He leaned over and flipped open his Swiss Army knife and stabbed at the ground impatiently. More sandy dust was dredged up. He continued the search, expanding the perimeter. And as he hacked away at the ground, he began to remember another time.

It was twenty years ago or more, he wasn't sure. The images were sporadic and mixed-up-crazy like, a jangled mess, patched together countless times with no care to order. He had nearly died a couple of years ago and he'd seen his life flash before his eyes and vanish, as if each frame of his personal movie had stayed too long in the light and was vaporized before his very eyes. Now scenes of his past rattled off before his mind's eye like an "edited for television" movie, with just enough scenes missing to make it interesting.

Manx remembered pushing his hands into the damp Redondo Beach earth. It was two-thirds dirt and one- third clay, so that in a rain it became the kind of mud that would hold you down. He'd lost a shoe once, left it behind in the mud, crossing the garden with an arm load of freshly cut vegetables.

Gawd! He thought. Had it been that long since he'd been up to his ankles in Mother Nature? He couldn't really believe that but he knew that it had been a long time. He really missed the dirt and its world of green shades and growth and death. He missed the taste of the dirt under his finger nails. He couldn't remember when they hadn't tasted like car grease or oil. He missed its smells: after a rain or when it was freshly turned up, like a new idea or an old friend.

He returned to the vacant lot; too quickly. His longing for dirt weighing him down, like two shovel-fulls on the chest. Surveying this personal archeology that had progressed during his recent mindlessness, he saw that he had dug a small oval into the sandy soil. It was about as big as a tub. The hole was a foot or so deep. It revealed only more sandy loam with bits and pieces of the city imbedded in it. Nothing else, at least, not what he searched in vain for. And this became a metaphor for the greater search that he had been on for months now, without even knowing it. His search for dirt was also a quest for a more natural way of living. He wanted to float away. He wanted to sleep in that garden again. Curled up among Bok Choy and Broccoli, Celery and Cabbage. He wanted to reach back into his past and pull out a handful of rich, dark, fecund soil; as alive with possibilities as the womb of Mother Nature herself. He stood up, savoring the mix of desire, nostalgia, and solitude; for it seemed to him that no one in this asphalt-loving town could share this dream.

Then he saw the other holes, and, as old as they appeared, he knew he was not alone.

FLAT TIRE

Manx hung up the phone. The call had not gone as well as he could have hoped. In fact, he felt a little like those two guys who tried to hold up that B of A in North Hollywood in '97: confused, disappointed and resigned to the fact that it was going to be a bad day. He suspected that he was being setup but all he had were his suspicions, no proof. The proof was in the pudding and the pudding was somewhere out there, beyond his grasp. He thought he wanted the "pudding", but that was a younger man's game. He knew he'd be lucky if he could get the attention, much less the affections of any "pudding", tasty or otherwise. Oh well.

In his day, well, to be honest, he had never really had a "day". Phrases like "Coming into your own" or "When your ship comes in" didn't seem to register in his reality. They were foreign concepts like a balanced budget or a football team *ever* taking up residence in L.A. again. He smiled at this. It wasn't often that he smiled, but he smiled on life more than it smiled on him. Small consideration.

Women and cars were a strong theme in his life. By the time he got a hold of them, they were on their last legs, which meant that he was usually stuck with 'em after they broke down and stopped working all together, or they turned out to be more expensive than he could ever afford.

He'd always had 'luck with the ladies', but it was mostly bad. Oh sure, sometimes it would work out for a while, but mostly it was like going to the DMV to renew your license or register a car; there was always that damn line and some piece of paperwork that you forgot to bring . Women were like that. All that potential, but first you had to wait in line, then prove that you were worthy, and then? Some little piece of information would prove to be inconsistent with your story and *BAM!*, you'd be out on your ass again.

Now, as the conversation with the potential "pudding" was deteriorating, Manx found himself dreaming of a bicycle. Maybe he'd get one with training wheels. Probably wouldn't hurt as much when he ran into the next brick wall...

FEAR MOVES TO A NEW TOWN

Manx sat across from the La Salle, enjoying his coffee as he opened his mail. The morning sun was doing its best to cut through the chill of early winter. It was not very successful. Every so often, someone (probably some drunk) would let out a scream from across the street. It was natural. Life is a truly scary proposition these days, and the shock of living it would make the most sane among us cry out if we hadn't been conditioned since birth to do otherwise. As he contemplated this (and the swirls in his cappuccino) a youth, of passing acquaintance, sat down (uninvited) at the table and began to rant.

"Truth is a broken mirror. Justice is an empty box. Intimacy is a suicide note. Desire is an empty shot glass."

Your point being...? Manx thought.

Was this really news to this kid? The world was neither safe nor sanitized; yet every time you turned on the box there was some government stooge trying to convince you otherwise. Likewise, every time you went out there was some goon preaching righteous indignation from a makeshift pulpit. Or some kid who had just discovered that life sucked, preaching to the choir at some poetry 'reading' or in some alley where the 'chronic' burned and spoiled dreams mingled with spilt booze. He wondered where these people had been? How had they missed the decline and fall of practically everything sacred?

The kid was on a roll now. He knew it and Manx knew it. Trouble was, he wanted nothing to do with the kid. The kid brought out a fear that had plagued him for years. A fear which he had learned to suppress by ignoring it. A fear that had gone unnamed for years: homo-phobic. *Not as in* homo*sexual* fear, but as in homo-*sapien* fear.

He looked at the kid. He wished he could make the kid disappear... forever. He wondered what would happen? Could he get away with it? Would anyone notice? According to the kid, no one gave a damn if he was ever heard from again. Manx drifted into a murderous daydream of doing vile things to the kid (just to show him how bad it could *really* get) before dropping him head-first down a mineshaft out in the Panamints, or maybe, over by Pinto Basin.

"Truth is a handful of dirt. Justice is the open grave."

A scream punctuated this statement. Manx lurched forwards out of his chair, his letters scattering like bystanders at a drive-by shooting. His hands clutched the kid's throat. It was soft and innocent like a Harp seal. He choked out the words as Manx brought down the club.

"Beauty is getting what you wished for... whether you like it or not."

"Too true, too true;" thought Manx.

He was long over-due for a change of scenery, anyway.

OLD ROCKING CHAIR

Manx rinsed and spit, watching the pink swirl move towards the drain. Looking into the mirror, he wasn't pleased with his new look. Forty-nine miles of bad road stared back at him, hard and cracked like the remnants of route 66, pockmarked like old Anaheim Blvd. (down by the harbor). Forty-nine miles of bad road and every mile was a year long. The whites of his eyes were framed with a watery red line that reminded him of the dawn's early light and tiny red veins meandered out towards the pupils like lazy bolts of lightning. The lower eyelids looked like two fat-bellied burlap snakes digesting a full meal. A liver spot was developing on his cheek, spreading like the slick from a leaking 50 gallon drum of oil.

His eyes began to ascend toward the top of his head, almost out of self-defense, but there again lay more trouble. Like his beard, which was more salt than pepper, his hair was showing signs of wear and tear.

Manx cocked his head back a little, catching the light on selected hairs. It reminded him of a field of rye, around October, kind of leaning to the north. Scattered across this field in a random pattern, silver slivers of light glinted back at him. These were no longer mere gray hairs. The 'silver years' were settling in.

The phrase, "Male Pattern Baldness" suddenly materialized in his mind's eye. He felt a tinge of envy. Other men were going bald in their early thirties, their hairlines receding like noonday shadows. Why was he cursed with a full head of hair?

Well, if he was going down *that* road, he knew he'd have to leave off going to work, because *that* list of 'whys' was long and always ended somewhere around "why was I born in the first place?" Sometimes he got all the way to "why were my parents even born?" But that was rare. Today he got as far as "why am I even going here?" He sighed and stood up.

His chest was a mottled white and little red dots moved across it like a horde of county jail day-laborers swarming alongside the freeway on trash detail. A cluster of hairs huddled together further down as if his chest was trying to decide if it was done with puberty or not.

He glanced down at his feet and saw only the tips of his toes or at least the fuzzy outlines of them. A checklist materialized and 'glasses' was near the top; not far behind, lurked 'penile implant'. Manx shuddered. "Maybe I'd better start taking that 'DongCry' before my dick stops working." He hadn't seen his dick in quite some time anyway, so what did it matter? It was original equipment, and, so far, it worked fine, did all the things it was supposed to do. Maybe it took a little more concentration sometimes, but Manx never needed any help when he was with company. Thank God for that little bit of mercy. He sighed.

POINT FORTY FIVE

The mind is a strange and wondrous contraption. For some unknown reason, Manx had a strange taste in his mouth. Something in the air by the Union Oil Refinery had triggered the old memory and brought that acrid taste of blue steel and machine oil back to him, like a dog returning with a stick.

There's really nothing quite like the taste of a gun barrel; the barrel in question here, being attached to his father's Colt .45, semi-automatic pistol; the famous WWII model that was *the* standard for many years, for the private collector.

He was freshly arrived at his father's apartment, a recent graduate of both his mother's house and the fine institution of higher learning known as high school. His father, himself a recent graduate of the same house, was ill-prepared for the joys of raising an eighteen year old man-child. They were strangers, quartered in an old apartment building by the beach, just a stones throw from the Scattergood Steam Plant.

He had managed to fulfill his obligation to society without cashing in his ticket, but now, in the post-school, pre-job dawning of his manhood, he struggled with the demons of his despair nightly. Four years of abuse at the hands of both his mom and the school system had pretty much taken their toll on him. He was a loner and alone in his exile, under the dis-trustful and judgmental eyes of his father.

He'd dreamed of going to Art Center and studying painting, but daddy backed out of the deal, drawing on his massive knowledge of the art world and his son's gullibility.

"You're not good enough." And Manx had believed this.

His mother had tossed him out without so much as a 'see ya!' He'd come home one day and found his belongings piled by the front door with a note scrawled across the cover of The Beatles White Album, laying on top. "GET OUT!" And that was that.

Manx tried to spit the bitterness out of his mouth. It didn't work.

Back in those days he figured he'd get used to the taste of the barrel, get used to squeezing the trigger so he wouldn't jump and make a mess of the thing. Then he'd put the damned clip in. It was a dirty business and he wanted to do *something* right before he moved along the Karmic wheel. He'd seen how the Buddhist monks immolated themselves on the streets of Saigon and thought; "now, that's class!" But fire made him horny and this didn't seem like a proper state of being to exit from the living. He was so naive in those days.

He wanted to slip away from life. He wanted to ease into a nice hot tub and just get paler and paler until he was no longer visible. Until it no longer mattered. He figured that no one would miss him. Or maybe they would and it would be too late and then they'd really feel bad for making him suffer. But he didn't believe that his going would make *anyone* that upset. *He* was the one who was most upset with the idea.

So each night, when his dad would go out to seek his own brand of solace down at Duffy's Tavern, Manx would prepare his "tableau of death", which consisted of some candles, a black sheet and the gun. He'd kneel on the floor, pop out the clip, eject the round in the chamber and very deliberately place the muzzle of the weapon in his mouth. Then he'd wait, as if he was really taking his temperature. After a few minutes, he'd slide it in farther, until it lay flat the length of his tongue. He didn't find out about the psycho-sexual implications of this act until years later during a therapy session. He merely knew that he got a thrill out of caressing the gun barrel with his tongue.

Manx never did put the clip in. Before he could get up the nerve to do it, he found something else to put in his mouth. He never looked back at those dark days until much later in life and, only then, on those days when the taste of steel would return, mysteriously. Only then could he slip away, for a little while.

* * *

EL PAGANO

"**P**lease, mister, let me show what the name of pleasure is."

Her breath smelled of cocktail weenies and decay; tooth or moral, I couldn't tell which.

"Show me your tits!" I demanded.

She slouched down in the front seat of my Plymouth Duster and fumbled with her top, succeeding, finally, in pulling it up to her chin. Her left hand was crippled and it made her work harder than most. I liked her spunk. I hoped that she'd like mine.

Her tits were nice. I reached over and fondled one of them as I drove along. It was firm and responsive as I rolled the nipple between my finger and thumb. I appraised the breast as if it were a ripe avocado; good texture, not too bruised, probably would taste good with a squeeze of lemon and a dash of garlic powder. Yeah, she'd do very nicely.

"Mister, I like to swallow," she whispered with her putrid breath as she tugged her shirt back down.

"Fine. I'll see if we can't find something for you to gargle."

"Huh?" She was fumbling for something in her purse.

She seemed high or demented or both. She was certainly stupid. Life had worked its magic on her and reduced that magnificent brain into a primordial squirrel cage; blunted it into a dull throbbing organ that recognized only the grossest desires: food, fear, sleep and greed.

"I got to get high first, then I'll really show you somethin'...;" her voice trailed off as she nodded out.

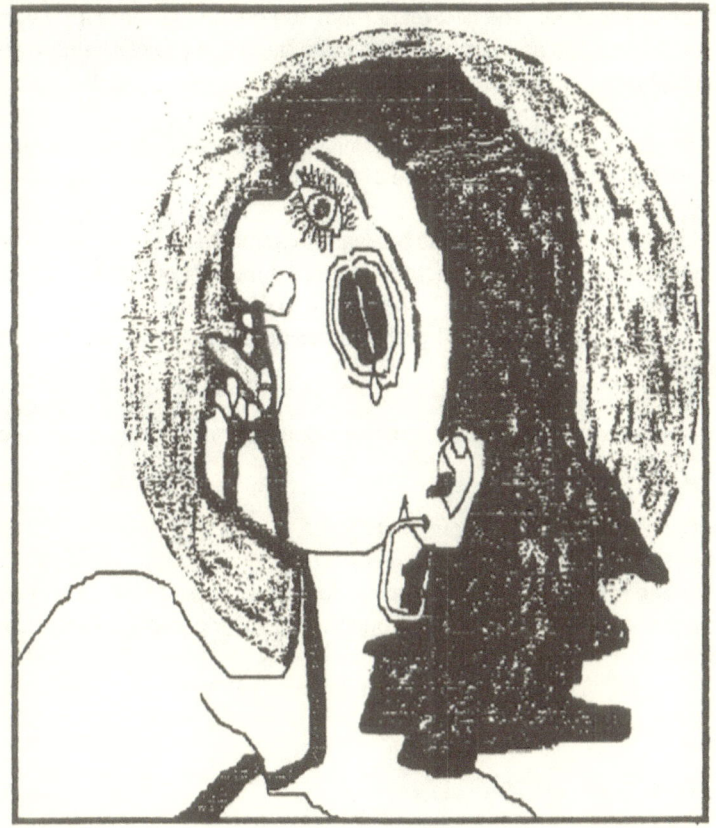

Raindog

I drove to a friend of mine's and scored a balloon for her. He owed me a favor, but I still had to promise him a piece of her ass. What did I care. He could have whatever was left over. I would use the dope to lure her from the car into my pad. Which I did.

She looked pretty comical stumbling up the steps, what with her bad hand and gimpy leg. I had sunk pretty low. But, hell, it was an easy slide down to the bottom of the barrel; what was that old saying? 'The longest trip begins with the first fall?' Or something like that. Anyway, she was hypnotized by that little bag of joy that I waved in her face, and it called to her, pulling her on, upward. I don't think she even knew where she was, or cared, for that matter.

Once inside the house, I told her to park it in a chair. I kept an eye on her as I got a candle and some matches.

"Here, help yourself;" I said, handing her the balloon.

She pulled out her works and prepared the spike. The dope gave off an acrid odor as it melted. She tied-off her arm and began to search for a vein, flicking herself. Then, like some monster from the depths, a snake-like tube surfaced and she stabbed it, a modern day Ahab.

Thar she blows! I couldn't help chuckling to myself. I may be a sick, sombitch, but, at least, I still had a sense of humor!

Her head lolled sideways as the warmth spread across her. She looked up at me, her head in profile. I thought of Matisse, I thought of Picasso, I thought of an old girlfriend named Denise. This whore could be Denise! I was suddenly gripped by the need to know! I grabbed her purse and dumped it on the floor beside her.

"Hey! What the fug are you doin...?" She muttered, trying to raise her hand in mock protest.

"Shut-up and take off your shirt!"

As she tried to comply, I searched for her ID. I picked it up and squinted at it, trying to make out the letters through the yellowing plastic. It was very hard to decipher.

"What's your name?"

"What're you, a cop!?"

"No! What's yer name? It's not Denise is it?"

"Not if you don't want it to be.." she muttered.

God! It couldn't be!

"Were you born in Switzerland?"

The whore gave me a dirty look that changed to wonder.

"Hey! How'd you know that?"

Geeezus! It was her!

Denise. I'd lost track of her years ago. She'd had some awful times, done some really stupid things in the name of 'love'. She'd told me some really hair-raising stories about her dad and his pals, about some of the fishing trips he used to take her and her sisters on. She'd shown me a scar she got from grabbing a fishing hook when she'd lost her balance one time while he was "teaching her about loving" as she used to refer to there little sessions on the boat. The scar!

I looked at the topless figure in the chair. Grabbing her hand, the bad one, I flipped it over, palm up, and scanned the thumb area. There it was. It was unmistakable; because the fishhook had stayed in her hand for several days before he'd had the courage to take her into the Doctor's. The scar, a hook-like impression in the skin. God!

"Denise!"

No response.

"Hey!"

"Wha...say are we gonna fuck or what?"

Maybe I was wrong. Maybe it was just a coincidence.

"Yeah, sure, okay, sorry, it's just.."

The words to an old Tom Waits song ran through my head.

I started to unzip my pants. As I did, I remembered how Denise used to give me head; always in a rush like she was drowning and my cock was a snorkel tube, or something. I got a hard-on just remembering those days gone by. My whole life began to wash past my eyes, sickening me to see where I'd come from and what I'd become. A rank hustler, about to use an ex-lover like the cast-off piece of jet trash she'd become.

The whore saw my meat waving in my hand.

"Oooh! I want some of that, please? Let's have a taste, ok?"

And she was trying to pull me over to her with her feet, hooking her toes into the crook of my knee and pulling her legs up, drawing me closer. And I, in my confused nostalgia, moved closer as she rubbed her breasts with both hands, cupping them and fondling her nipples, desperately, somehow; her mouth open-ing up to receive the piece of salami that I held in my hand. And then, she was on me, her hands working in a frenzy to free my belt and drop my drawers to my ankles. Almost mechanically, she parted her lips and slipped my swollen rod into her mouth. And equally as mechanically, I began to slip into the old rhythm, grip-ping her by the hair and sliding in and out, while she worked her tongue along the shaft.

Damn! It *was* Denise! Nobody gave head in such a distinctive manner! I'd come across a few who came close, both male and female, but nobody ever did it like this! A wave of nausea swept over me. If she hadn't been so good, I'd have gotten sick. But she was GOOD!

She slurped greedily away at my prick. Her hand worked the shaft, sliding the skin back and forth, just like I'd shown her, some twenty years earlier. She sucked me into her mouth, pulling my cock in until her nose hit my pubic hairs. Then, she'd grab my ass cheeks and knead them as she twisted her mouth around on my shaft like it was some kinda candy cane and she was trying to suck the stripes off! Goddamn! She was good!

"Goddamn, baby! Oh Yeah, suck it! Suck the life outa me!"

She was moaning, too. We were both getting close.

I looked down at her nipples. They were hard and pointing upwards towards me. I reached down with one hand and pinched one really hard. It was automatic. It was what had scared me away from her in the first place: her desire for more and more extreme sensations. I squeezed it so hard, I was surprised it didn't just pop like a grape! She gasped, half in agony and half in ecstasy! I pulled the breast towards me by the nipple. Denise let out a moan, more animal than human. She began to rub my cock across her face, as if she was trying to erase the abuse of years, as if my cock was a big, pink art gum eraser that could, somehow clear the cobwebs from her brain. She was trying to remember something, but it was useless. Her brain, that is.

Suddenly, I stiffened, my breath coming in short, hot snorts. I grabbed her head with both hands and pushed my trembling cock up to her mouth. She grabbed it near the base, squeezing it tightly, and, with her mouth open wide, flicked the head with her tongue, snake-like. Her eyes widened as I tried to force it into her mouth; but she held me at bay with her hand and a new-found strength.

"Je taime, baby, je taime!" I purred through my clenched teeth.

I convulsed as my load rocketed into her mouth, like love's own firewater! She wrapped her lips around my pulsing rod, as wave upon wave of jism sprayed into her, her tongue lapping it up, greedily, working as fast as the bucket brigade in Fantasia.

At last, it subsided, and pulling my cock from her mouth, she laid it against her forehead while she lapped up the creamy ooze that flowed along the shaft, down to my balls.

"Ah, Denise, you old cow, you haven't lost your touch!"

"Say! Don't I know you?!"

I looked at her through my tears and could see that the cobweb curtains had drawn back enough for her to make some sense out of all this, at last. I looked down into her eyes and saw that old look of demented, unfocused anger. I saw it but I couldn't move fast enough to do anything about it, until it was too late.

Denise grabbed my cock, twisting it hard before popping it back into her mouth and biting down. HARD!

I yelped like a castrato! I yelped and tried to back away, but she had the strength of a pit bull! Instinctively, I slapped both hands onto her ears. She howled in pain and I slipped out of steel trap! Then, something took over inside me, like a fugue of rage. I can't explain what happened next.

I hadn't raised a hand to *anyone* in over twenty years; yet I beat her with a vengeance that sickened me, a vengeance that penetrated the darkest, most cynical and jaded corners of my own dulled psyche and shined a light as bright as any sun, exposing me so that even a blind man could see me for the miserable wretch that I had become. It was, in my book, a truly hateful and cowardly "crime of passion".

Denise lashed out at me as best she could, but could only muster enough strength to deflect a few blows with her skinny, rubbery arms. As time moved into a ballet of slow motion, they seemed to undulate like the tentacles on sea anemones. She pushed me backwards and I stumbled to the sink, my pants twisted around my ankles, tripping me up.

Instinctively I cupped my penis in my left hand and stared in disbelief at the welts running parallel along its base, teeth marks forming a dotted line, indicating where to tear. Behind me I heard the chair going over as she angled herself towards me, a look of pent up, demented rage contorting her face even more. She lurched towards the counter, towards a knife that was laying on a plate waiting to be washed. I waited, the bass drum of my heart pounding in my ears, drowning out the sound of the molecules as they crashed into the ear drum's outer skin.

In slow motion, you have a little time to think about what you are doing. There is a strange detachment from your actions, as if you were watching a movie, as if it wasn't about you at all, but was about someone else's hand grabbing the iron skillet, tightening around the handle, feeling the course metal dig into the soft skin on the palm. It was as if someone else's stomach muscles were tightening, coiling like a spring, about to unload this pan into the face of the enemy.

I watched as the hand suddenly jerked up, the force of the pan spinning me around, turning me into her path of fury, catching her square in the face with the bottom of the heavy, iron skillet. She is stunned by my sudden move. She drops to her knees with a telling finality. Her eyes, one swelling closed already, follow me as she slowly collapses onto the floor. Only her eyes turn, nothing else. If it weren't for her eyes, I'd think she was already dead.

There's a thudding sound as she hits the floor. I hear her moan. She rolls her head sideways and searches for my eyes. Something is very wrong. Her eyes zigzag up towards my face but I can tell that they will not stay focused. Her mouth is slightly open, bleeding, lips swollen, a tooth broken off just above the gumline. Blood is forming a sticky pool around her head, like a halo in one of those sixteenth century icon paintings. Her nose appears to be trying to turn her face around further as if she's trying to look over her shoulder. The nose is broken, pressed flat against her cheek, and blood pours out of it like holiday drivers escaping from the city.

She reminds me of Picasso's "Guernica". The way her head is twisted to the side, her broken teeth and twisted mouth, she is as beautiful and as terrifying as the tortured faces of the horse or the mother, grieving for her dead child.

There is another moan followed by a gurgling sound.

I stare at the frying pan in my hand. There is a faint misting of blood on it. I drop it back into the sink. It falls with a clank. I can't seem to get time to speed back up. I sink down to the floor, my naked ass not even feeling the kiss of the cold linoleum. Her eyes are struggling to stay focused on me. You can almost sense the light dimming, winking out, never to be re-lit. A numbness begins to lap gently at my feet, slowly progressing up my legs, a black, inky kind of oblivion mercifully obliterating her meandering stare, swallowing her completely, the way she had swallowed me only moments before. And then the blackness swallowed me too.

Alone in the fading light of dusk, I watch the smoke as it wafts upward into the silence of this room. I can scarcely move. My life has suddenly gotten very complicated. Implications and regrets are mixing with memories, the gravity of this situation pulling me down, rendering me incapable of reason or movement. Denise is dead; laying on her red carpet, staring through me and off towards Avalon.

I, too, am dead. At least, I think I am. I can't seem to move, can't seem to feel anything; can't act, can only re-act. My brain feels like a thick layer of mold has grown over it, as if it has crashed. I am only vaguely aware of the cigarette as it begins to burn too close to my fingertips, only vaguely aware of the throbbing between my legs.

I must shake off this malaise. Got to clear my head.

Staggering towards the bathroom, peeling off my clothes as I go, I step into the shower and turn on the cold, only. The anticipated shock of ice water is missing. I won't be springing into action this time. I've dug a deep, deep hole this time and no clever, quick thinking is going to get me off the hook. This time, it won't be so easy. This time, I'm gonna need to come up with a really clever angle to save my sorry ass.

Standing under the spray of cold, harsh reality, my head begins to clear and I begin to hatch the plan that will work. I don't believe there's a chance in hell that I'm going to pull this off, so it becomes a game, of sorts, to see how long I can elude the inevitable collapse of my little empire.

At first, I can't accept what's happened in the last few hours. Then, the litany begins as a somewhat maternal voice begins the third degree inside my, still woolly, head. Why the fuck did I let her get into my car in the first place? What was I thinking? Was I crazy? Or just plain stupid? Stupid with lust for those tits and that mouth! Thinking with the wrong head! It's time to start thinking with the right head! Got to clean up this mess, clean up this life, got to move. Move! Stepping out of the shower, I turn on the hot and leave it running, as I walk back into the other room, naked. Bending down, I tense as I pick up Denise, expecting to lift a dead weight. I'm surprised at how light she is. I cradle her in my arms, her head lolling away from me, the eye that's not swollen shut surveying the room as I turn and carry her into the bathroom. Her blood trickles down her breasts and forms a sticky reddish-brown syrupy line where my flesh meets hers. As I carry her, the smell of her rises to my nose. It's the stench of slaughterhouse death. It reminds me of the dead pig caresses I saw through an open doorway off of Jack Kerouac Alley. That was San Francisco, many moons back. Denise weighs about as much as one of those pigs. Is this merely a bag of bone and gut and muscle and blood to be disposed of like so much trash in a dumpster? Or does she deserve more?

Denise, or what's left of her, slips gently out of my arms into the tub. Her head, arms and torso lay over the edge, the cascading water, like hot rain, cleansing her wounds, her matted hair, as I work to free her legs from the rest of her clothing. Once stripped, I ease her down into the tub, completely, step into the thin red soup and sit down at her head. The hot rain pisses away my tears as I begin to clean Denise's wounds. Pulling her head up to my chest, I wash away the blood from her breasts and belly and farther down. Lovingly, I wash every part of her, amazed at my tears, amazed at this sudden flood of grief that rises out of me from some forgotten place of memory, perhaps from our time together before, or other times; I don't even try to figure this one. I pull her to me, cradling her like some stupid kitten that's just died, rocking her limply back and forth, as God's own tears wash down on us.

Afterwards, as I'm drying her off, I take inventory of her other traumas, experienced at the hands of the brutes before me. I am the biggest brute in her short life, the final brute. The walls begin to close in as this realization sinks in. I must stay focused, I think to myself. I've got so much to do before...I'm not sure what is going to happen next, but I've got a plan unfolding in the back of my brain and I know from experience that auto-pilot is best right now, just living on instinct, right now.

"Trust the force, Luke!" Obi one Kinobi counsels.

Denise is laying on my bed, on her back. Her body, from head to toe, is a road map of dead veins, bruises, scrapes and burns. There will be a great sadness along Pacific Avenue when the word gets out that everybody's favorite rag-doll is gone. Denise, who had worked this street for at least two years, was kicked around worse than a junkyard dog. Her only saving grace, apparently, was the dullness of her brain, which stayed focused on the prize: the almighty greenback! She was a wreck, but she could still suck. Well, she used to be able to suck, at any rate.

As I patted her dry, I remembered what a fucked up sexual dynamo she was when I first met her. She could take on two or three at a time. It didn't matter what hole, she was very accommodating. I also recalled that she looked, walked, oozed and tasted of sex most of the time, but was always kind of uptight about it at home. But, oh, how she loved to fuck in front of strangers. And outside, God, how she loved the Great Outdoors!

One time, we were driving up to the Bay area, up the newly opened Highway 5, when we got caught in a terrific downpour. It was so heavy that we had to pull off the highway. So, we're sitting in the cab listening to the rain pounding on the roof of the car and all of a sudden she's all over me like a cheap suit! The next thing I know, I'm standing outside her open car door with an umbrella and my pants around my knees, in the middle of a monsoon! I had to fuck every orifice at least once before she'd let me get back in the car! She was nutty about fuckin' and she was makin' me fuckin' nuts!

And now, I had killed her. I probably put her out of her misery, judging by the scars on her body; but was that my right, my decision? Wasn't it really up to fate and the Gods? Of course, fate had put us together, so maybe I was acting as an agent of God!

"Geezus! Get a grip on yourself...an agent of God's plan, his holy design? Come on, son, have you forgotten who you see when you look into the mirror?"

My conscience made a convincing argument. I went back into the bathroom and double-checked the mirror, just to make a reality check. Yep. It was definitely me and not Mother Theresa. Mother Theresa would never end up in this kind of a bind. But then, as I thought about it, she probably wouldn't have strayed so far off the "right" path, as I had done, either. In fact, Mother Theresa would probably be leading the pack that was gonna come after me...especially if I did-n't get my ass in gear!

I opened the medicine cabinet, reached down and dumped out the trash can and scooped all the contents off the shelves—I'd sort it later. Next I moved to the toilet, reached into the tank and pulled out the 9mm that I kept in there, just in case (and to conserve water), inside a waterproof zip-bag that I'd gotten from a guy I used to know at the DEA. I dropped this in the can as well.

I pulled a duffel bag out of the closet, filled it with clothing and dragged it into the living room. I couldn't be in the room with her. I had to stay focused. I needed a plan. How was I gonna get rid of the body? I liked the idea of explo-sion and fire, mayhem, but I knew that modern police methods would easily detect the slightest discrepancy and I could never afford the freight on one of them high profile shysters. So, what? I needed a fall guy, a pigeon, some guy stupid enough to let me set him up. But who?

I dressed as I thought. I cleaned up the kitchen as I thought. I drank a beer, smoked a cigarette as I thought. No one came lumbering into my head. Which was odd, since I am normally ass deep in stupidity. All the guys that work for me are sub-normals, but I liked them all, in their stupid little ways and this job required that I picked someone that I neither liked nor disliked; which, in my line of business was pretty tough, since I basically either liked or disliked everyone I knew and vice-versa.

I wandered back into the bedroom and stood at the foot of the bed. Denise looked sorta angelic laying there in the twilight. She looked so fragile and virginal and at the same time, there was something, probably her nudity, that made her look almost sultry. I started to get a little horny, but that meant going too far!

Geezus! What's next? A trip down to the mortuary for a good, stiff one?

And then it came to me. Oh yeah! My buddy that still owed me a favor was gonna get a chance to free his debt, once and for all.

My buddy knew a guy who actually worked at a mortuary preparing the dearly departed for their last moment in the public eye. We called him the Goon. What made the Goon so special (and I'd been hangin' on to this little tid-bit for quite some time, just waitin' for a situation like this to come up) was that he was a necrofile! He was a freak that liked to do it to dead bodies! And, he was about my size; and he was the nephew of a guy named Big Frankie! Big Frankie was lookin' to take over my end of town, had been waitin' for a few months for me to slip up. Tonight, I was gonna slip up, big time!

I called my buddy up and, despite his protests, offered him a deal that was too good to pass up. He finally agreed, but I had to promise him the moon on a silver platter. He agreed to make the call and bring me the supplies I needed to carry this off. I got to work.

First, I surrounded the head of the bed with candles, like an altar. Next, I sprayed air freshener until I began to choke on the stuff. Okay. The stage was set, now I needed to get to work on the grand finale!

My buddy showed up about thirty minutes later. I gave him five grand and he gave me a light bulb and two, five gallon cans of Methyl-Hydra-something. He wanted to come in, but I knew the old saying about ignorance.

"Listen, the less you know about this the better!"

"So when do you want me to call the old man?"

"Give me about an hour."

He turned to leave and then he turned back.

"Hey man, good luck."

"Yeah, right, I'll see you in Hell!"

"Heh, heh, yeah, not if I see ya first!"

I closed the door. The Goon would be showin' up real soon, so I had to get busy. I opened up one of the cans and stashed it in the empty closet in the bedroom. Then I hauled the other can down to the garage, opened it and poured some of the liquid into a couple of glass jars and a plastic milk jug. Then I poured a little out onto the "work bench" I'd built in another lifetime when I'd worked with my hands. Now, I worked with my mind and the only work that the old bench saw anymore was when I was leanin' against it, talking on my cel-phone, workin' a deal! Finishing up, I got up on a ladder and knocked out the false floor in the closet, which was just above the back door in the garage. I needed a stash box for times when unwanted members of law enforcement dropped by, unannounced. The heady aroma of potential brain damage wafted down to meet my nose.

"Thank God that shit's heavier than air;" I muttered to myself before coughing into my sleeve. I nearly fell off the ladder.

I got back to the bedroom, having turned off most of the lights in the house. I unscrewed the bulb in the ceiling, pocketed it and screwed the bulb that my buddy had brought with him. This was a special kind of bulb that was able to convert standard 110 into something, really quite extraordinary! It was like a magnesium flare wrapped in napalm. A bright light, a big bang, enough inflammable liquid to level this building...it would be pure poetry, a glorious, white-hot streamer straight to the Devil's door step! Just me, her, the Goon and the old man; such a deal!

The Goon showed up ten minutes later. He was all in a lather. He was anxious...and sweaty. I hesitated before letting him in the door. This guy was SCUM with a capital SCU! How could I let him defile Denise? I paused for a moment, guilt flashing across my conscience. My God! I'm pimping for a dead woman! This brought a whole new meaning to the term "getting laid".

Fuck it. Denise would probably get off on the idea! But just to be on the safe side, I told the Goon to give me a few minutes with her, alone.

"Hey, I thought she was dead! I ain't interested in no play acting bullshit with no actress!"

"Hey, hey, settle down, settle down! Here's a drink. Believe me, she's as dead as they get!"

"She ain't stiff yet, is she? 'Cause if she's stiff, I sure as hell ain't payin' no five grand! Hell, I can get that kinda action at work!"

"Don't worry, I just want to make my peace with her before you start in on her."

"Well, okay, but don't take too long, I got a stiff comin' in later tonight and I gotta get back to work in an hour."

His dedication was touching. He was the backbone of the economy. I hoped that the economy could continue without him. Time would tell. Time never knew when to shut up.

I closed the door partly and moved over to Denise's side. It was three hours since this sickness had begun. It seemed like I had been living for this hour, and the next few hours to come, for a long time. I hoped that it was gonna' be worth it.

"Denise, honey, I'm sorry about what's happened. I'm even more sorry about what's gonna be happenin' to you next. I'm gonna be with you real soon, so don't you fret."

I took hold of her hand, not even being bothered by it's coolness. Denise stared at the closet door out of her one, "good" eye. She knew what was going on, I could tell. There was a certain reassuring serenity in the air. It gave me the confidence and the courage I needed to carry out the next part of this little drama.

"Get ready." I whispered to her.

"Okay, pal, let's see the color of your money!"

"I need to see the merchandise, first, to determine it's quality;" he stated flatly.

I was startin' to hate this guy, which was not good. I was gonna have to break the one rule in my code that I never liked to break: never mix business with pleasure! Oh well, it wasn't like I had much pride left, anyway!

"Okay, but leave the light off, I'm trying for some 'atmosphere'!"

"What-mos-phere? Heh, heh, you kill me man!"

He moved towards the door, opened it and peered inside. His body tensed and he spun around, whipping out his "roll" and tossing it to me.

"Whoa, Geezus God-almighty!" He hissed through clenched teeth. "It's all there, let's get on with this!"

He had already started to undress, as he said this. I moved towards the door. He followed. Once inside the bedroom, he finished stripping and just stood at the foot of the bed, getting ready. He had a jar with some kinda greasy lookin' white shit in it and he was scooping out handfuls of this and smearing it all over his penis. I should say, his slab of meat! He had the biggest cock I'd ever seen, at least on a white man! It was like he had a third forearm stickin' out. Damn! It was big! No wonder he had to fuck the dead! The dead couldn't complain.

"Big isn't it?" He said, as if he could read my mind. "Too big for the living!" As if he *was* reading my mind!

He puts down the jar and moves around to her side and begins to touch her, almost lovingly, but with this club-like thing sticking out in front of him.

"Oooh, head trauma! Do I have to pay extra for that?"

Is he serious? This Goon thinks he's gonna violate my Denise!? I don't think so!

I slip out the door to my duffel bag and get my gun, load it and head back in to protect the deathbed of my beloved.

He's forcing his meat in between her legs when I walk through the door.

Turning towards me, he gives me a nice view of his enormous, purplish cock descending into her cool, ice-blue freshly scrubbed cunt.

"Where'd ya go?" He asks.

"Went for a cold one, want one?" I reply.

"No thanks, got one..," then he grunts and laughs.

Then he begins to pump her, slowly at first, then faster and faster. I can't believe what I'm seeing. I'm watching a guy fuck my ex-girlfriend who has just died! The guy who killed her is now watching her get fucked by a guy who likes to fuck the dead and who is about to join the ranks of the dead himself!

The Goon was getting pretty rough. He was pretty tough around the dead. A real macho dude! I wondered how tough he was going to be in a few moments. He'd be pretty tough after the firemen found him.

As he grunted away, nearing the completion of his sordid little task, I positioned myself across the room and waited, silently, in the dark. I raised the gun and aimed it at the back of his head. Across the room, he was just getting off, arching his back and holding that position for just a moment before slamming into her and spitting his hot load into her dead box.

"Oh geeeze!" He cries as he collapses onto her.

POP!

The neighborhood I live in is so used to the sound of gunfire that even the dogs don't get upset unless you plug one of them!

Sorry, Denise.

"Franklin, are you okay?!"

The voice comes from out in the living room. It's the old man! My hair stands on end and adrenaline spikes through me like lightening strikes on an Omaha-prairie August night! Now the real work begins. So far it's been like a dress rehearsal. Now, the real test begins!

I jumped across the room and stepped behind the door, which opened slowly, almost on cue.

"Franklin? You in here? I got a call...it's Uncle Frank. You okay?"

A big head attached to a big set of shoulders leaned into the room. Big musta run in the family. The old man was searchin' for the light switch, when the scene caught his attention. An explosion of ideas roared across his mind's eye, almost knocking him over! The Goon lay buck naked, with his meat buried into some broad and there was all that candle crap, like an altar or something and how was the old man gonna explain *all this* to his priest, and...

"What the..."

Frankie had frozen in his tracks. The broad on the bed was *staring* at him! His left hand waved in space, trying to flip on the light switch, but he was a good two feet from the wall. It was now or never. I swung down as hard as I could.

WHACK! Another explosion caught him just behind his left ear, succeeding in knocking him over, this time. Big Frankie collapsed to the floor like a brick facade during an earthquake! I reached down and pulled his piece outta his big hand, as big and brown as an old mitt. It was a nice old snub-nose .38 that had probably been a family heirloom, passed down from punk to punk. I dropped it into my pocket and squeezed his fingers around my 9mm. It looked like a water pistol nestled inside his big, old paw.

Suddenly, he grunted. I jumped backwards. He was still alive. So was I.

I grabbed my stuff and hit the alley walking fast. My buddy had stashed a car for me a couple of blocks away and it was right where he'd said it would be, full tank and all. It cranked over when I hit the key and soon, I was heading up the hill to Lookout's Point, where I could keep an eye on the sleepy harbor town below. From my parking spot on the Lookout, I could look right down on my place, about half a mile away to the south.

Big Frankie tensed as he came to and immediately started coughing. The fumes were awful! Rising to his hands and knees, he struggled to get his bearings. His head was pounding as if it had been slammed in a car door! He staggered to his feet, tried to open the bedroom window, failed, and headed out to the kitchen, where he succeeded in opening a window.

Franklin, my son, what have you gotten yourself into now? He thought as he surveyed the scene in the bedroom. He'd seen enough dead bodies to know that the couple on the bed wouldn't be going out dancing later. But what the fuck was that strange smell? And who'd slugged him? Big Frankie's brain was starting to fire on all eight again, his animal instinct sensed imminent danger. Warily searching the darkened apartment, his eyes squinting to penetrate the gloom, Big Frankie reached over to pick up his piece off the floor. It felt odd in his hand. Looking down at it in the candle light, he casually reached over and flicked on the light switch.

BUH BUH-BOOM!

The cool night silence was suddenly punctuated with several loud, thudding booms. Down in the darkened hollow, about where my place was, a huge, broiling mushroom cloud of fire and thick, black smoke erupted. This was followed quickly, by the sound of car alarms, shattering glass and about a thousand excited dogs. Then, there was another explosion, followed by the screaming and shouting of the survivors.

Ah, Mayhem! I thought as I turned over the engine and headed north.

Three down, one ta go.

I drove until I didn't recognize the street names, figuring no one would recognize me for a while if I stayed in an unfamiliar part of town. I still had to clean up some loose ends before I could disappear. For one thing, I had to pull in outstanding debts without calling attention to the fact that I wasn't really dead. For another, I had to plan my escape. With the fifteen to twenty grand that was floating around with my name on it, I could leave the country, if need be, so I had to do some fast juggling to get free and clear.

I found a little motel near the truck stop off highway one-fifteen, with just enough turnover for me to blend in. I stocked up on groceries, so I wouldn't have to be seen in public, and began making phone calls. Sometimes I'd use the celphone and sometimes the phone in my room. The first call I made was to my friend, the lawyer. He was very relieved that he hadn't lost my retainer. I was touched by his sentimentality. I'd decided to let him do most of the legwork for me. He was more than happy with that arrangement, since he was now in the driver seat of my little empire. We agreed that he would pull together as much of the money as he could and then meet me somewhere. I smelled a rat. The phone receiver almost stank of greed when I hung up, but I had to rely on him for a little while and then...who could say what might happen? I still had the old man's .38. I watched the morning news report about "Mystery explosion rocks harbor area town", but the cops didn't seem to know much about it, or they weren't saying much. Besides it was in a part of town that was known to be infested with drug labs. *Good!* I thought; *they think that it was a 'meth' lab!* Unfortunately, the explosion took out about half the block. Apparently, there was a chain reaction and several labs went up. In the confusion that followed, a number of innocent bystanders were killed, either by shrapnel from the explosions or by gunfire that broke out when the fire department showed up. Apparently, I had started a minor riot. I'd better get all the money from that scumbag lawyer...I'll probably have to shoot him, too.

Suddenly, I was very tired. So, I slept.

The telephone woke me up. It was dark in the room, but it felt safer, I was less exposed. I lit a cigarette and answered the phone. It was the lawyer. He was gonna need a couple of days, I gave him until noon tomorrow and said goodnight. I packed up my shit, loaded it into the car and headed east along the foothills. They coulda been tracing that call; I had to play it safe.

Around noon, I found myself in a little industrial town surrounded by gas lines and oil derricks. The men all had that hard-edged look that comes from hard labor and hard luck. A gas jock recommended a place down the road, where the rates were cheap and the questions, few.

Checking into this joint was too easy. They hadn't asked for any ID or even a deposit. The clerk at the desk was a sweet faced lad who'd, somehow, managed to sidestep most of life's little mishaps. He would've given Andy Hardy a run for his money. He assured me that this was a "family business" and that their motto was, I swear it's true, "Don't bug us and we won't bug you".

I pulled into the back, found the room, started to reach for the door, when it opened by itself! A young woman, blond, in her twenties, dropped her cleaning supplies on the floor as we surprised each other! She quickly bent over to pick up her stuff.

"Oh golly! I'm so sorry! I'll have this cleaned up as soon as I can." She was referring to a bottle that had broken.

I watched her work. Her cleavage suggested that she had some nice tits inside her dress. Generally speaking, she looked pretty good. I was surprised that I could even feel anything after last night's little party, but here I was getting horny for the housemaid.

After she had finished cleaning up, she hustled off and I unpacked, again. The room was cool and dim, with the curtains pulled shut. I left them that way. I stacked my groceries in one of the cabinets beside the bed. I was agitated. I knew that my lawyer would be cutting a deal with the Man if things got too hot. I had enough money with me to stay underground for a couple of months, but I didn't want to spend two months looking over my shoulder. Maybe, I should just head for Portland or something. I had a cousin up there, once. She might still let me in the door, if I played my cards right. First, I needed to get a new deck, though. This one was about played out.

Again I laid down on the bed and took a nap.

Someone was tapping on my door. TAP, TAP, TAP.

"Sir? Sir? I'm sorry to bother you, but I didn't finish preparing your room. Sir?"

"Just a second, justa second," I said as I staggered over to the door to make sure she was alone. She was. I opened the door, stepping back into the darkness, away from the afternoon sun that crept in through the doorway, ahead of her. I could see her silhouette through her dress as she entered the room. I turned away from her, partly to hide my erection, and partly to make sure that there was nothing incriminating visible in the room. She busied herself with dusting. I tried to avoid looking at her as she moved about the room. She was making me very hot. I wasn't sure if she knew it or not. *I've got a few hours to kill, I might as well test her.*

I laid down on the bed, carelessly, kicking off my shoes. She turned around to see what the noise was. She looked at my shoes, then scanned along the length of the bed, looking at the body of a tired man. She saw the bump in my pants, but it didn't appear to register with her what it meant.

"Long drive?" She asked, standing next to the bed.

"Yeah."

"Where'd yuh come from?"

"Pear Blossom."

"Pear Blossom? I've been there! How was it?"

"It was one whore's town."

"Yep," she laughed, "that sounds about right!"

"Listen, when do you get off...from your shift," I asked (Goddamn, I wanted to get in her pants!)?

"In about an hour, why?" She looked at me mischievously, as if she knew the answer already. Her eyes had drifted back to the middle of my body.

"Is this your last room to clean, before you get off...of work?" I asked as I reached down to unbuckle my belt.

"Could be," she said in a distracted voice, biting the edge of her lip as my hands worked on the snap and began to pull on the zipper. I stopped and waited. She stepped to the edge of the bed.

"I thought we could have some fun, you and I," I said as I pulled the zipper down all the way. "Maybe, I could give you a reason to come back after work, you know, a little incentive."

"Like what?"

"Like this!"

I reached over and grabbed her by her shoulders and pulled her towards me. My lips were on hers, pressing them flat, pushing them apart so my tongue could leap into her mouth. At first there was a slight resistance, but that quickly faded and her lips came to life. She opened her mouth and her tongue invited mine over for a wrestling match. I pulled her onto the bed next to me and did a quick check for concealed weapons, all in one smooth, continuous motion. Everything seemed to be in order. I was still wrestling with her tongue, when she reached into my pants.

"Lose something?"

"I'm looking for my tip," she stated deadpan.

"I'll give it to ya when you come by after work, say six o'clock?"

"Okay."

TAP, TAP, TAP.

Six on the nose. I liked that. I checked the peephole to make sure she was alone. She wasn't. There was another woman with her. I opened the door a crack.

"Who's yer friend?" I asked.

"This is Betty, she likes to wrestle, too. I thought you might like to watch us!"

Hmm. I opened the door and let them in. They sat on the bed. Betty produced a bottle and took a long pull off it. She seemed a little edgy. But, after the next pull, she seemed to open up a little bit. She passed the bottle to her friend who was already undoing her blouse. She took a big hit and handed it to me. I took the bottle, leaned against the credenza and took a swig. It burned. I looked at the bottle. The label read: Old Rot Gut. Figures! Setting it down, I turned to watch the two of them wrestle.

Betty started first. She reached over and slipped her hand into "blondie's" blouse. She felt around until she found what she was looking for and then she began to rub it back and forth. Blondie sucked in some air and hurried to get her blouse opened; then she kicked off her shoes and socks. Betty flipped open the blouse and continued to knead the breast and nipple. She leaned over and tipped Blondie's head back so that she could give her a kiss. Their lips met, parted and tongues emerged, tentatively greeting each other. Soon, they were wrestling intently with each other. Betty's hand moved down along Blondie's skirt and, upon reaching the hemline, promptly made a U-turn and headed north. Blondie's legs shot apart, allowing Betty's hand to reach in and grab a handful of muff. I thought Blondie was gonna swoon. It was getting hot.

"Say girls, it's getting kinda hot in here, you don't mind if I get a little more comfortable, do you?"

They were too busy to say anything, but Blondie gave me the "OK" sign as she flopped onto her back pulling Betty over onto her. I took this as a yes and peeled off my shirt. Then I unhooked my belt, unzipped my pants and stepped out of them. My boxers stayed on but my erection was very obvious. I took another swig from the bottle. It burned less.

Meantime, Betty had dropped to the floor and was pushing her head in between Blondie's legs. Blondie got up on her elbows and looked down delightedly at the head bobbing up and down between her legs. She smiled, rolled her eyes up into her head and then looked in my direction.

"Give me a taste, handsome," she said gesturing for me to come over.

I picked up the bottle and brought it over to her. She poured it into her mouth, over her lips and down her chin. Betty stopped muff-diving, rose up on her knees and began to lap up the booze as it trickled down her chest. I reached down and lifted up the hem of Betty's skirt and ran my hand over her butt, the muscles flexing into tightness at my touch. My cock wanted to breathe, so I took it out and stroked it a few times. It stood up, proudly, saluting the girls. Blondie tapped Betty on the shoulder and pointed in my direction. Betty looked back at me, shrugged and went back to giving Blondie the licking she so richly deserved. I backed up to the credenza and slowly began to stroke my penis, up and down, up and down. This was not lost on Blondie, who was still on her elbows, watching me. Soon, she was pushing Betty back down between her legs, partly, I think, so she could have a better view. Blondie's lips began to curl up in a snarl, kinda. Her breath came fast and hot. I noticed a fine misting of sweat forming on her brow. She was close. I could go for a while longer.

Just then, she pulled Betty by her hair, roughly drawing her up onto the bed, sucking, loudly, her own sweet juice from Betty's mouth and lips. Blondie rolled Betty over, pinning her to the mattress. She began to beat her with hands open, slapping her face and chest, Betty's arms flailing in a failed attempt to ward off the blows. I merely watched, still stroking my cock.

"You fuckin' cunt! You're no better than anyone else in this town!"

I didn't understand what was going on. But I liked it. My cock got harder. I stopped rubbing it and just let it stand out there in the breeze, pulsing slightly. I heard something rip and I looked over at the couple on the bed.

Blondie had torn open Betty's blouse and was pulling off her bra. Then she looked over at me. The anger on her face melted away to a smile as she stared at my throbbing tool. Then she pulled the collar of Betty's blouse together and raised her "friend" up. Betty's face was somewhat bruised and she winced as she rose. Blondie shook her hard.

"Look at it!" She demanded, but Betty refused. "Look at it, you fuckin' lesbo!" But Betty would have nothing to do with me or my member. So what, at least Blondie was interested. She dropped the cunt licker and stood up on the bed and unhooked her skirt. She kicked it at me and missed. Then, using her foot, Blondie raised Betty's skirt, revealing her underwear. It was obviously wet. Blondie stood over Betty's head and suddenly dropped onto her, spreading her knees at the last moment, just missing Betty's head. Betty just lay there, having suffered through this before, apparently. Blondie began to grind her cunt into Betty's face, slowly but deliberately, to the left and then to the right. Soon, she was grunting and groaning. She was good. If things were different, I'd take her to a friend of mine over in Vegas, she'd be making the kind of money that bad girls always want, in no time at all. But, things weren't that easy now, except for the next few hours.

Just then, Betty's hands kinda fluttered up, poetically, like dry leaves picked up by a little breeze, and began to roll her panties down. I reached over and pulled them off for her. She didn't seem to mind. The hands fluttered up towards Blondie's breasts. She leaned over to meet them. The hands gently caressed the breasts, massaging them and their nipples. I noticed that one of the nipples was pierced with a ring about the size of my index finger. As I watched, Betty found this ring, slipped it over her finger and began to pull on it insistently, guiding Blondie's face towards her cunt. Blondie tried to resist but, she couldn't do much, except look up at me pleadingly. I stared back at her and watched as Betty's legs spread apart. But Blondie wouldn't descend onto that cunt, so I obliged Betty by stepping between her legs and kneeling down, prepared to insert my cock into her throbbing pussy. Blondie stopped resisting and reached over to spread Betty's pussy, tickling her clit with her index finger and dropping a big wad of spit right on target!

I inched a little closer and pointed my cock at Blondie's mouth, that full-lipped, drooling orifice, her tongue extending to lick off the sap as it dripped out.

"Here's yer tip, sweetheart," I said.

She smiled and leaned forward to accept it into her mouth, looking up at me as she did so.

"By the way," I asked, "What the hell is yer name, anyway?"

"Thunneece."

"Say what?"

She let go of my cock for a second and began to massage it with one hand. She looked up at me again and said, "Denise."

She pulled me back into her lips and I began to fuck her mouth, rougher and rougher. She began to twitch her cunt again and I could hear her starting to come. I pulled my cock out of her mouth and lowered it towards the pussy. Denise smiled through her coming and parted the lips of Betty's glistening pussy. Denise pushed her tongue over Betty's clit, the tip of it extending to the edge of the opening, where she could touch the shaft of my cock as I pushed it in. Which I did. Much to Betty's chagrin. She protested but Denise held her down and, once I got up to speed, soon she had her legs clamped tightly around me, savoring the ride, instead of merely enduring it.

I was getting close. But I wanted to fuck Denise in the ass, just like in the old days. So I stopped stroking and pulled out.

"Wha...what'er ya doin'?"

"I don't wanta waste my sauce on some lesbo! I wanta fuck you, while she sucks you off!"

"You mean..?" Denise's eyes got bigger.

"That's right. I wanta fuck you...in the ass!" And so saying, I took another pull on the bottle and moved to the other side of the bed.

Denise was trying to raise up and protest, but Betty was holding her tightly, now, and wouldn't let her up. Her little ass was twitching back and forth, but somebody's tongue was melting her defenses.

"Gimmie some of that pussy juice!" I said as I roughly jammed my meat into the spot between Denise's legs. I don't know what I stuck my rod into, but it was hot and wet and both women were starting to buck. A couple of quick thrusts and I withdrew, my cock greased and ready to plunge into the tightest hole of all! I placed my hand on the small of her back and pushed downward, pushing her pussy into Betty's face. As I did this, I placed my prick against her anus and began to slide it back and forth between the cheeks of her ass. She began to relax. Sensing this, I positioned myself and pushed the head inside her. She bucked like a horse!

"No, please! I'll do anything you want! I swear! Pluh, pluh, please don't duh, duh do that! Please! Betty make him stop! Oh, Betty I'll do anything *you* want! Make him stop!"

"Shut the fuck up!" I growled, as I leaned forwards and pushed her face into Betty's cunt and held it there until Betty could get her head in a sort-of scissors lock! Then I let go and began to pump her in the ass, slowly and deliberately. Denise continued to protest, but her moaning eventually diminished to a kind of grunting as I pumped her, my rhythm beginning to pick-up speed.

"Unh, unh, unh, unh, unh, unh, unh..."

Betty's hands began to pound the bed and grab the sheets, pound and grab, pound and grab and she came, her cries muffled by Denise's body. As soon as Betty let her legs relax, Denise was up and pulling away from my dick, yanking it out of her ass and spinning around, dropping over Betty's leg and frantically rubbing her clit against it. I stroked my cock a few times and blew a load into Denise's face, mouth, tongue. The jisz dripping out of her mouth and into Betty's mouth and face. Then, she reached over, grabbing my dick and sucked the rest of it outta me, bent over and licked up all that had spilled onto Betty, rolled it around in her mouth, and, while she straddled Betty's chest, looked me in the eye and spit it right in my face!

I punched her right, square in the mouth! She bounced over backwards and rolled off the bed onto the floor. She was more startled than hurt I think. I doubt if anyone had ever done that to her before. As near as I could tell, she'd been asking for it for a while. She stumbled to her feet and grabbed for my jacket as she lost her balance. She pulled it to the floor with her. I looked down at Betty. She looked up at me, past my cock and mouthed the words *thank you*.

"Well, well, well, and what do we have here?" Denise was rising from the floor holding something in her right hand. She raised her hand and, shakily, pointed the .38 at me. It was cocked.

I backed off the bed, my hands extended at about shoulder height, elbows slightly bent.

"Now, just hold it, don't do anything that you're gonna regret for the rest of your life!" I was moving towards her slowly, as I talked, trying to lull her into lowering her guard, so I could grab the gun away. I thought, *now I'll have to tie the two of them up, maybe take one of them as a hostage, but which one, maybe Betty; naw, I'd have to take the little spitfire!*

Just then I heard the spitfire say, "Don't you come another step closer, I mean IT!"

I inched closer. I was almost there. Almost.

BANG!

It was slow motion time again. Both girls screamed as I staggered back from the force of the bullet, as it slammed into my guts. It was an old fashioned bullet, it only went in and buried itself in my guts somewhere; never exiting out the back like these new-fangled teflon coated things! I don't think she had really planned on pulling the trigger. But, it was too late now. My life was beginning to ooze out a little, pinkie sized hole. My new navel was leaking!

They grabbed their clothes and began to dress, quickly. In the panic, Denise had dropped the gun on the bed. I grabbed it and waved them out the door. Then I stumbled over and locked it. I pushed a chair up under the door-knob, just for added security. Then I pulled my pants back on, grabbed a towel off the floor and held it to my wound. It turned red, slowly. I sat on the edge of the bed, fumbled with a cigarette, got it lit, inhaled deeply and waited. It wasn't a long wait.

I could hear them coming down the walkway. At least two pairs of angry feet, heading my way. I waited, checked the remaining chambers of the gun, *five to go.*

BOMP, BOMP, BOMP! The door rattled from the knocks. Good, solid, square knocks; the kind that you deliver when you're feeling particularly righteous! I aimed about four feet from the floor, right smack in the middle of the door and waited. The handle jiggled but didn't give!

"Open up in there! Mister you'd better open this door right now, because you have some *explainin'* to do! I don't know where you're from, but around here we take rapin' our sisters very seriously!" It figured that one of them would be his sister.

This guy has been rehearsing this speech for too many years! I thought. So I shot him.

Judging by the squalling howl of pain from the other side of the door, I'd say I pegged him, but good! I heard some muffled shouts and some groaning and then it got real quiet, again. I reached for the bottle and took a swig, forgetting every "gut-shot" scene from every cowboy movie I'd ever seen! It didn't hardly burn at all until it got to my stomach and then it felt like I'd swallowed napalm! I doubled over and then, mercifully, blacked out.

I awakened to the sound of soft, feminine voice, gently speaking to me.

"Je taime, mon ami, je taime."

"Denise? Is that you? Where are you? Oooh, owww, ohhh," I groaned as I sat up, startled.

It was darker, so I flopped back down and reached for the reading lamp by the bed. As I looked over for the switch, I thought I saw headlights floating above me on the ceiling. But as I watched, the lights changed into a shape, gossamer-like, which changed into a ghostly image of a woman. She looked a lot like "Venus" except that her head had that awful "Guernica" pose. She began to descend until she was just overhead. She turned her head so she could see me out of her one, good eye. It was as I had expected, Denise had come for me.

It was weird. I had never seen a ghost before, and yet I wasn't afraid of her ghastly visage, or even horrified by my impending demise. I was sorta serene, I was okay with the idea! I was okay and yet, I felt a great sadness wash over me like a shockwave and tears began to plummet from my eyelids like Lemmings. Regrets began to appear in my minds eye and then fade from view, appear and fade, appear and fade, appear...

I felt this sudden need to atone for my sins, as if Denise could hear my con-fession and with a wave of her pale and diaphanous hand, forgive me. I knew that once that was done, the last chain that bound me to this world would be broken and I would go to...somewhere, I didn't know and didn't really care, I just wanted to get on with it!

So it began.

"I never expected to end up here, in this town, dying under these cold, nameless peaks, where they only know me by the alias I used at the desk; I never thought that I'd end up being shot with my own gun, or that I'd ever even own one or many, or for that matter, that I'd ever become so used to violence that it would come to me as easy as scratching my ass. I was a very different man when I knew you last, when we walked the beaches and dreamed about Paris and the acade-my, and how we were going to make it work this time because we were different. I had a dream and I was going to make my little world a better place. 'Teach by doing.' Gandhi had written, and I had every intention of doing that, by living a simple, yet focused life. I never sought much in material wealth, I 'lived simply so that others could simply live!' I made sacrifices in order to continue to live in my enlightened poverty. Yet, somewhere along the way, I got lost. Somewhere along the way, I let my greed and avarice overwhelm my conscience and ethics. As I got older and older, the options for living on the edge of society got fewer and fewer. The process of living 'right' and still living by your wits became more and more stringent, while I became less and less conscientious and dedicated. I'll have to say, here, too, that getting fucked over so many times, I've lost count, was a *minor* incentive towards the *'Road more traveled'* , you know what I mean?"

Denise hovered silently, over me, her left hand covering her breasts, her right hand slightly extended, as if she was waving hello (or good-bye).

"And I hadn't even noticed just how callow and empty my life had become until yesterday when you re-appeared in my life! And just as quickly you were gone again, only this time it was forever!" I was suddenly bawling like the lone-somest loser in the world! All my days of lost causes and lame decisions came rushing back over me like the waters of the Red Sea over Pharaoh's army. Scenes with no emotion at all, flashed before my eyes in a random pattern that began to accelerate and made me dizzy.

I opened my eyes, not remembering having closed them, and Denise was leaning close to me, smiling angelically. Her hand was poised just above my heart. I felt very safe.

"Is it time?" I whispered.

"Oui, mon cher."

I looked into Denise's face and it began to evolve to another face. It was the face of Denise, some twenty-five years ago, when I'd first met her, when our innocence was a gift and not a weakness. It was the soft, supple and passionate Denise that had first trapped me.

I parted my lips to kiss her, as my eyes welled up with tears and I felt the touch of her hand on my heart.

"Then, take me, now."

Denise's hand closed around my heart and held it, loosely, like a dying bird, not wanting to crush it, but just to hold it. She held it until it stopped beating.

*   *   *

Marshall Astor

About the Author

RD Armstrong is a fictional character living in a 'dime' novel world. He prefers to adopt this persona in order to spare his family any humiliation that might otherwise befall them. Aside from his obvious lack of a moral compass (he attributes this to years spent at the bottom of the barrel studying the denizens of Slackerville and Bohemia) or even the ability to discern up from down, Raindog (as he is known by many) has carved out a niche in the alternative small press as both poet and philosopher. In other words, he can sling shit with the best (and worst) of them.

He has been published widely in both print and on the web. His book credits include **Fire and Rain** *selected poems 1993-2007* (volume 1 & 2), **On/Off the Beaten Path** *the Road Poems*, **Roadkill, Last Call: The Legacy of Charles Bukowski, Bone, The San Pedro Poems, Pedro Blue, In Memoriam, The Hunger,** and **Paper Heart**.

If the reader requires further explanation visit his website, where all will be revealed: www.lummoxpress.com